Fragile CREATURES

by
KRISTINA CIRCELLI

http://www.circelli.info

Copyright © 2014
Cover by Michelle Monique Photography
Editing by Juli's Elite Editing
Formatting by JT Formatting

ISBN-13: 978-0976372868
First Edition: January 2014
Library of Congress Cataloging-in-Publication Data

Circelli, Kristina
    Fragile Creatures/Kristina Circelli – 1st ed
    1. Fragile Creatures - Fiction 2.   Fiction - Young Adult
    3. Fiction - Contemporary

For Duke and PJ
the giraffe and goat who forever hold a
place in my heart.

AWAKEN

SHE AWOKE TO the harsh sting of fluorescent bulbs and the bitter scent of sterile air that were home to just one place — the hospital.

A white wall met her vision first, then a cheap plastic table with wilted blue flowers atop it, and, finally, the sleeping form next to the bed. For a moment she could only observe the woman, sleeping deeply yet fitfully, her head resting on a propped-up hand in a way that looked horribly uncomfortable. The woman's clothes were wrinkled, her hair unwashed, face swollen with the evidence of many, many tears.

She tried to speak, to call out *Mother*, but soon found that any movement was too much for her broken body to bear. So instead she allowed sleep to take her again, preferring the solitude of dreamlessness to the reality of what she would face when she awoke once more.

"EASY NOW," HE said, his voice gentle to quell her rising nerves. "Turn gently, let the wheel slide through your hands."

She followed his voice, each movement matching his softly spoken words. A successful maneuver, one that awarded her a smile and pat on the shoulder.

"Nice work, my little elf," he said, his nickname reaching her ears with affection. "Just go with the flow," he directed, settling back in the seat. "One car length behind the one in front."

The road took them on a silent journey, each concentrating on thoughts not spoken. Her — delight in overcoming fear, joy in the feel of such freedom. Him — compassion for the young girl's nerves, pride in her courage.

"What's next?" she asked, eyes trained on the road before them.

"Beep-beep-beep."

Confusion filled her, tearing her eyes from the road. The world around her disappeared save for the haunting expression on her passenger's face, its foreboding threat shadowing the golden morning sun. "What?"

He faced her, eyes dark, reflecting some frightening thought he couldn't voice. He pointed one thin finger at her heart. "Beep-beep-beep."

There was something different about his voice, something mechanical. It frightened her. "What are you doing?"

She started to reach out to him, comfort him, save him, but he pulled back and smiled. "It's time to wake up now, my little elf."

TIME HAD PASSED since she last took in these walls, this sterile scent, those heels clicking down the hall. How much time, she didn't know, but her body had been given a reprieve from the pain at long last. She could have slept longer, given her wounds more time to heal, if not for the unrelenting hand that forced her awake. The face that stared down at her wasn't familiar — it was cold, harshly lined, masked.

The face of a stranger.

Then another appeared, quelling the panic that threatened to rise in her chest. Familiar brown hair in loose, if not messy, waves, familiar porcelain skin, familiar blue eyes that sparked with both worry and a hint of something she couldn't identify — or perhaps didn't want to.

But, no matter the expression, she knew this woman and reached out to her, confused by the hesitation, yet grateful for the clammy hand that eventually clasped her own. "Mom," she whispered, surprised by the roughness of her voice. It wasn't her voice, normally so cheery and light. This one belonged to a stranger, someone who had experienced the kind of despair not soon forgotten. "What happened?"

The woman — *Mother* — sat down next to the bed, brushing a hand over her daughter's gaunt and pale face.

There was something rough about the gesture, not the gentle caress the girl had been expecting. "There was an accident … sweetie," the woman spoke the word as if it pained her to do so. "You're in the hospital. You've been here for two weeks."

Accident. Hospital. Two weeks. The steady *beep-beep-beep* of monitors that insisted she wake from a dream she couldn't remember.

"Evangeline?" Her name was spoken by the unfamiliar face, a nurse who peered down at her with kind eyes. The mask had been removed, giving the now not-so-unfamiliar figure a friendly face. "Can you tell me who you are, your age, the last thing you remember?"

"Evangeline Lorelei Frost. I'm sixteen," she answered, hazel eyes drifting from one woman to the other. Her voice still disturbed her, so foreign and unforgiving. "I remember …"

Let the wheel slide through your hands.
One car length behind the one in front.
What's next?

"Where's Dad?" she asked, feeling an unwelcome tightness deep in her chest. "I remember we were in the car. He was giving me a lesson. Where is he?"

The women didn't answer. They didn't need to. The tear that escaped down her mother's cheek before she caught it was answer enough.

WHEN SIX MONTHS PASS

THE THOUGHT OF facing endless looks of pity, condolences that were only half believed, kept her in bed beyond the start of school. Just one day among them, among the pitying expressions betrayed by accusatory eyes, broke her more than she thought was possible. Worse than their looks, though, were the whispers. Whispers of the life she'd taken, whispers of the mistakes they thought she'd made, whispers of the mother she'd destroyed due to a grieving heart. Strangers, some genuine, some choosing to forego friendship, projected blame onto the girl and continued their misguided judgment, even when she refused to entertain their gossip.

Her body had healed since the accident that stole her father's life, but her mind — that was still very much broken. There was no redemption for what she'd done, and so she accepted her punishment accordingly — the limp in her right leg after shattering her knee, the scar along her left cheek where glass had imbedded itself, the stiffness in her right-hand fingers due to broken bones. Once, she'd been considered a rising talent in the art community, but the accident had left her barely able to hold a brush — another punishment she accepted without complaint.

"You're late," a hard voice called through her door. The tone sounded bored, almost encouraging listeners to ignore it.

Evangeline waited until the footsteps retreated down the hall before forcing herself out of bed. That voice was yet another fear that kept her in bed, the only place of comfort she had left. Cruel, often distant, no longer kind … Greeting its owner became more and more difficult with each passing day.

Her morning routine was quick — dressing in yesterday's jeans, pulling her unbrushed auburn hair into a loose braid, and slipping on years-old flip-flops. It was early fall, but South Florida afforded her at least that one luxury. And flip-flops were her luxury, for such simple things made her happy despite the pain she now lived with. The warm weather supposedly helped her wounds heal, though these days, Evangeline rarely ventured outside. Too many people, too many whispers. Too many reminders of what — who — wouldn't be waiting for her when she returned inside.

She found her mother in the kitchen, hunched over the morning newspaper with a coffee mug in hand. Pausing in the doorway, Evangeline took a moment to observe her. Edith Frost had once been a beautiful woman, the kind that turned heads as soon as she entered a room. But six months of mourning had hardened otherwise soft and delicate features; grief had set in the lines around her mouth and eyes, listless indifference now apparent in the way she held herself. Evangeline supposed others would still find her attractive, but to those who knew Edith best, this was a woman lost in sadness.

I caused that, Evangeline thought, eyes casting downward to the floor as a wave of depression swept over her. She'd caused her mother's turmoil, and there was no forgiveness for that.

Sensing another's presence, Edith looked up, dark hair falling across unpainted eyes. The shadow of a grimace ghosted her lips before she turned her attention back to the paper. "School started already. You're late. Again."

"I know."

"So get going. It's a long walk." When her daughter didn't respond, Edith looked up again, this time catching Evangeline with a hardened gaze. "Are you deaf now too? I said get going."

"Sorry," Evangeline whispered, picking her messenger bag up from the floor by the kitchen counter. Her knee protested the move, threatening to buckle, aching enough that she released the bag, knowing she wouldn't be able to carry the extra weight if she had to walk. "Can … can you drive me?"

Edith took a sip of coffee. "You'll walk. Consider it physical therapy for the injuries you caused yourself."

Evangeline stood still for another moment, considering. Once, in another life, her mother would have jumped at the chance to drive her, savoring every minute she got with her daughter to chat about their days. Sometimes they'd even play hooky, hitting up the beach for a day of sun or the theater for a secret movie marathon. But the days of having her mom as her best friend were over.

Evangeline pushed herself forward, out the door. She didn't carry anything, not even her wallet. Her books were lost somewhere in her bedroom, or perhaps her locker at school. A tutor had visited her at the hospital and later at home to help her keep up so she wouldn't have to repeat any grade, but always brought the needed materials. Evangeline never cared where they came from or where they went after she was alone again.

Outside she stayed close to the inner edge of the sidewalk, hands in her jacket pockets, hood obscuring her vision. In her seclusion, she could almost pretend the world around her didn't exist, that her isolation was chosen, that her life may have still held meaning if she decided to push back the hood and embrace everything she used to love.

But deep down she knew the truth. With each step on the cracked cement, each deep breath and sharp exhale, Evangeline knew there was no salvation for someone like her.

Salvation.

Forgiveness.

The bitterness in her mother's eyes.

How long had it been since they shared a laugh? A hug? She never considered herself an overly friendly person, but once, long ago, she'd tried to be. The girl who tried to be liked, to fit in, to be someone others could respect — that girl was a stranger now, as foreign to Evangeline as a smile on her mother's face. Perhaps they no longer had anything in common, nothing that bonded them together like their father once had. They would live as roommates rather than mother and daughter.

The quick yip of a terrier snapped her out of her reverie. Evangeline couldn't help but offer a half-smile at the small, white-furred dog that pawed at her ankles. "Mr. Maximo," she greeted warmly, momentarily forgetting the dark thoughts passing through her mind. She'd always loved animals. Even on her darkest days, when sadness or annoyance or depression threatened to take over, an animal could always cheer her up.

"How are you this fine morning?" Somewhat stiffly, she lowered herself to the sidewalk, having to keep her bum knee as straight as possible. She allowed the dog to crawl over her legs, amused by the dirt and grass tangled in his fur.

"Oh, dear. I'm sorry, Evie," her neighbor called, rushing from her yard. Evangeline looked up to see the old woman hurrying over, still wrapped in her bathrobe. Her short white curls bounced around her face, giving her an interesting mix of elderly and youthful energy. "He's dug himself a hole under the fence and I can't seem to keep filling it fast enough."

That explains the dirt, Evangeline thought, running a hand through Mr. Maximo's fur. "It's no problem, Mrs. Jessup. Me and Mr. Maximo are old friends, aren't we?" She held the dog up to her face and rubbed noses with him, the hood of her jacket falling back.

In her momentary delight she didn't notice the way the old woman's eyes narrowed ever so slightly, the pity that filled them when she took in the scar alongside Evangeline's face. Such a harsh, unforgiving line that slashed down the girl's cheek and jaw — a permanent reminder of a day that could never be taken back, an act that could never be undone.

There had been talk of that day since it happened, hushed voices spoken behind cupped hands, whispers passed from ear to ear. Speculation was abundant, judgments made based on assumed facts; no one really knew what happened that day except for the one being judged, but those who whispered all agreed on one thing. The girl at the end of Lixon Lane was no longer the bright and beautiful artistic star of their neighborhood. No, she had become something else.

Broken.

Tragic.

Pariah.

"Shouldn't you be in school, dear?" Mrs. Jessup asked, pulling the girl out of her rare moment of joy.

A sigh was suppressed as Evangeline rose slowly, wiping her hands on her jeans. "I suppose so."

"It's a little late. Would you like a ride?"

"No," she snapped. Embarrassed by her display, Evangeline shook her head, pulling her hood back over her head. She attempted, and failed, a smile toward the old woman, who was staring at her with an uncomfortable amount of genuine compassion. "I'm fine. Thank you for the visit."

A RETURN TO UN-NORMALCY

FLUORESCENT LIGHTS. COLD tile hallways. Echoing footsteps. Only the lockers lining the walls and the papers littering the floor reminded Evangeline that she wasn't back in the hospital. The school should have been a place of happiness for her — it was the start of her senior year, after all — but the whispers, the looks, the silent accusations; such things were too much for one fractured mind to handle.

No one wanted her here. Evangeline didn't want to be there, could feel their blame. She'd been back to her high school several times since the accident, albeit rarely for an entire day.

Today would be no exception.

She found her statistics class after wandering the halls

aimlessly, peering at the latest locker graffiti and browsing flyers tacked on the corkboards, though she didn't really comprehend them. Parties and extra-curriculars were meaningless to her now.

Not that anyone would want her anyway.

Her seat was waiting for her when she stepped in the classroom, a single chair in the back next to the boy who used to be her partner in crime in their small Florida town. They'd been best friends since their days in diapers, siblings without the blood bond, mischievous kids always on the lookout for fun, but now he felt just as strange as the rest of them.

She didn't expect Cam to look at her when she eventually sauntered into the classroom, and didn't spare a glance to see if he actually did. Their relationship had changed since the accident, a barrier forced between them, threatening to sever the bond that once held them together. She supposed some of their forgotten friendship was an imagined discomfort, the result of their shared unfortunate circumstance, but she couldn't find the energy to find out if Cam still cared about her.

It was easier being alone.

If Cam or anyone else noticed her entry, Evangeline couldn't say. Though, she supposed walking in the door at the front of the classroom wasn't exactly subtle. Still, no one offered her a comment or lecture, so she sat in the back in peace, her mind focusing on anything, everything, other than the day she wouldn't let herself remember.

Sometime later, the bell sounded, a sea of students pouring into the hallway and leaving her behind as the lone island to face the impending storm. Almost alone, she realized, when she saw the silhouette of her old friend on the outskirts of her vision.

"Evie," that familiar southern-twanged voice spoke softly, so softly the single word may have been heard only in her mind. For a moment she thought she might respond, but could only keep her stare on her desk. Finally he turned away, though she sensed his hesitation before finally packing up his things and following the crowd into the bustling hallway. Part of her wanted to follow him, to talk through the tragedy that, in a way, they had experienced together. But getting up from the desk was too hard; speaking was too hard.

"Miss Frost," a deep voice said from the front of the room. Evangeline didn't lift her eyes to face the darkness bearing down on her, even when she felt its force calling to her, threatening her. "Miss Frost," the voice said again.

With a sigh, she dragged herself to the front, knowing when she looked up she would see a wiry face with high cheekbones and thin lips, topped with perfectly styled black hair. "Miss Frost," her math teacher said again, this time with more compassion in his words. "We've discussed this. You cannot expect to pass if you miss any more classes. I know things have been hard, but—"

"Hard?" Evangeline repeated, now bringing her gaze to meet his. "Whatever do you mean?" Her question brought forth a confused silence until he found his voice again.

"Miss Frost, I want to work with you. I want you to pass, and I can't sit idly by and watch you so eagerly walk the path of a dropout." The middle-aged teacher lifted his brow when he saw the sudden shift in her stance. "This is your senior year and I know you have it in you to overcome any troubles. If we work together, I'm sure—"

"Don't worry about it, Mr. Erwin," she cut in. "I'm perfectly fine being just another statistic."

With a half-smirk at her own joke — unoriginal as it was — Evangeline took to the halls. She remembered the winding passages fondly, and once enjoyed the throng of bodies that always ensured good conversation and even better laughs. Now it all felt foreign, an alien place — or perhaps she was the alien.

Outsider. Outcast. She could live with whatever title was bestowed upon her. She deserved it.

The back door to the art classroom opened before she realized where she was. This had always been her favorite place: a small storage room filled with art materials, with half a table shoved against the far wall. That table had been her workstation, and hers alone, for two years, with the paint smudges to match her creativity.

No one sat there now, though she heard evidence of another class in the room just outside her personal haven. Her little piece of sanctuary was waiting for her to return and so she went to it, resting in the uncomfortable wooden seat with its high back, running her hands over the stained and chipped tabletop. Many a lost hour had been spent here, dreaming of canvases and palettes, color combinations and textures. She had been given a great gift upon her birth, one that many admired and others envied, and that gift had once been her passion.

This table helped fuel that passion, tucking her away from the less serious art students, giving her a home away from home where she was free to get lost in her mind and bring her own kind of beauty to the world. Every paint smudge, every nick and groove in the wood, all were testament to an abandoned passion. Many of her old materials were still there: paint tubes tucked away on shelves, brushes bound together in holders, and even half-finished paintings still propped up on small easels that lined the back wall. As her eyes scanned those pieces of canvas stretched across carefully handmade frames, Evangeline wondered why her art teacher had kept them. None were commissioned paintings, but rather pieces born out of her own imagination. There was nothing inherently special about any of them.

Evangeline sighed, taking a lone brush in her right hand. The slender wooden shaft felt awkward in her fingers, unnatural. She mimicked a brushstroke on the tabletop, not surprised by the burn in her wrist or the way her pinky finger started to shake. The bones in her hands were mended as best they ever would be mended, but her grip wasn't the same as it used to be.

"It will take time to heal," the doctor had said during her first physical therapy session. "Your body has been through trauma, and will have to relearn tasks that were once simple. Give it time, Evangeline."

The brush slipped from her fingers and clattered to the paint-stained floor, forgotten.

AN UNSUCCESSFUL ATTEMPT

EVANGELINE DIDN'T REMEMBER walking home, but eventually she found herself in the kitchen, sitting in the chair her mother had vacated hours earlier. She was surprised to see that it was nearly five o'clock, but the time encouraged her to rise and begin searching the kitchen for ingredients. It had been a while since she cooked anything, since she and her mother had enjoyed a meal together. Perhaps today was the day they began to repair their broken bond.

It had been six long months since the accident, but those months may as well have been years for all the distance they put between mother and daughter. It began at the hospital, Evangeline waking up and seeing those familiar eyes staring down at her with worry and a hint of something that, to this day, the girl couldn't identify. Regret? Disdain? Anger? Edith's bitter tone betrayed her words when she spoke of well wishes, and when the police report had been made outlining the cause and result of the accident, that bitterness moved from tone to words. After six months of daily reminders that the accident had been her fault — a fact Evangeline didn't have the heart to dispute — she had given in to the truth that she would no longer have a loving relationship with her mother.

But, that wouldn't stop her from trying.

Soon the aroma of homemade lasagna filled the air. Evangeline couldn't cook many things, but lasagna she excelled at — and it had always been a family favorite. Many nights had been spent laughing around the table to plates of lasagna; Evangeline would bring those nights back. She cleaned while waiting for the meal to cook, hoping a good meal and spotless kitchen would inspire better conversation than their words earlier that morning.

Edith entered at half past six, only moments before the oven timer was set to sound. She paused at the scent of dinner cooking, casting a single glance in the kitchen before retreating to the living room. Leaning against the counter, Evangeline watched her mother take in the scene, not noticing the sparkling kitchen or place setting for two at the counter. Disappointment filled her when she heard the sound of clinking glasses and she knew that tonight, as nearly every night since the accident, Edith would pass the time with a drink in hand.

Her mother had once been bubbly and lively, always quick to laugh, the first to welcome a friend or greet a stranger. She loved spending time with her daughter, bragging about her artistic talents, staying up late to watch a movie or enjoy a little girl talk. Evangeline had been just as close with her mother as she'd been with her father. But that light had left Edith since the accident, when she turned to drink as therapy and shut out the rest of the world, her daughter included. Six months later, Evangeline suspected her mother had become addicted to numbing her sorrows with wine, just as she had become addicted to scorning the daughter who killed her father.

Her back straightened. No, tonight would be their night. They would enjoy a home-cooked meal together, side by side, even if they didn't speak a word. So decided, Evangeline waited patiently for the timer to buzz, then prepared two plates of steaming lasagna. Before the accident, they would often eat in the living room as a family, watching their favorite game show or the latest DVD release. Her father had loved to laugh, and often chose comedies as their dinner entertainment.

Tonight, they would eat as a family again, minus one.

She brought the plates to the living room and set up two stands, one in front of her and the other next to Edith, who was sitting at the far end of the couch, wine glass in hand. Evangeline noted the glass was nearly empty, the bottle on the table next to her half gone already.

"Eat, Mom," Evangeline said quietly, setting the plate down and gesturing to the food. "I made lasagna. Our favorite." Her eyes were hopeful when Edith glanced at the food, then at the television, which was playing a sitcom rerun. "I thought maybe we could have dinner together. You know, like we used to."

Edith was quiet for a moment. When she spoke next, Evangeline wondered if the words were said to purposely stab her deep in the heart. "Perhaps when your father is here."

Evangeline sank into the chair, toying with the fork in her hands. The rumblings of hunger she'd felt earlier when cooking had dissipated into a burning cramp, snuffing out her appetite. Her eyes were trained on the floor, her voice soft, when she replied, "He's not gonna be here anymore, Mom."

"Then I suppose it's pointless."

The words stung, more so than she thought they would. Evangeline took in a slow, deep breath, eyes burning with unshed tears, before looking up at her mother, but Edith was staring absently at the TV, food untouched. The silence between them stretched until, finally, Evangeline rose and brought her plate to the kitchen. Any joy she felt earlier at cooking had vanished.

She dumped the uneaten food back in the baking pan, then covered the leftovers with foil. Some part of her, a childish immature side, wanted to throw the whole thing in the trash, but she resisted. Perhaps later, if not tonight then tomorrow, her mother would welcome a meal together. And when that happened, Evangeline wanted to be sure she had food ready to heat up.

After the meal was put away properly, she retreated to her room. Only there did Evangeline allow herself one small moment of immature rage, rearing back and sending her fist through the cheap paneling wall.

A COLD HEART

"MISS FROST, YOU'RE wanted down at the office."

Evangeline glanced up from her desk, surprised. Mr. Erwin gestured toward the door, a slip of paper in hand that a student aide had just brought in. She hadn't heard the student enter, but then, she wasn't paying attention to much. She wasn't even sure where her notebook or pen went from the time she left for school to when she arrived in class.

At least I made it to school on time, she thought. Yes, that much she could be proud of. After her mother's quiet dismissal four nights ago, she had tried hard to be a better daughter, one Edith Frost could be proud of again.

So she'd cooked and cleaned, caught up on some homework and left it on the counter for her mom to see, and even went grocery shopping. It was hard, finding the energy to care, but she tried. Her father would have wanted that, and Evangeline would do anything to honor his memory. She would have done anything to have her mother hug her again, but she would take whatever she could get right now.

The hallway was cold and empty, greeting her with a mocking embrace. More fluorescent lights. More tile floors. More clicks of heels echoing in her mind.

Your father didn't survive the car crash.

You're lucky to be alive.

They said he died instantly.

"They were wrong," she whispered.

"Miss Frost?"

Evangeline snapped out of her daze, seeing that she was already in the front office. The secretary offered her a soft smile, a pitying smile, just like all the others. At least this one seemed honest. "Uh, yeah. Mr. Erwin said you wanted me."

"Yes, you can head on down to Miss Pearson's office."

A deadpan, almost satirical look crossed Evangeline's face. But she said not a word, instead turning on her heel and sauntering to the office she'd come to know well in the past six months.

They thought forcing her to that office would be good for her, a healthy break from the monotony of real life, a place where she could be open and honest with herself and others. They failed to realize that their *Miss Pearson* wasn't equipped to handle her kind of depression, her kind of isolation, and that trips to her office were merely more hurdles to overcome in her long, never-ending race back to sanity. She entered the room without knocking, taking a seat in the plush chair opposite a narrow wooden desk.

Picturesque landscape paintings, a softly bubbling fountain in the corner, zen gardens on the table next to her chair — the subtle touches were meant to make the ones sitting in her place feel anything other than what they were: troubled. She could hear the condescension in their very beings, inanimate objects sneering at the crazy, troubled teen looking in their direction.

"I thought you said we were done," Evangeline said before the woman could speak. Miss Pearson was a plump woman with a friendly, always smiling face. Her blonde hair was typically piled atop her head in tight curls and her dresses were always vibrant. Today was no exception, the yellow of her hippy skirt matching the color of her hair.

Rarely undone by a teenager's sharply spoken words, Miss Pearson only smiled. "I just wanted to check in and see how things were going. It's been a couple months since we last spoke. Some of your teachers have expressed concern—"

"I'm fine," Evangeline cut in. "I'm catching up on my work, promise. I just want to be left alone now."

"I spoke with your friend Cam yesterday. He said you were avoiding him."

The fact that the woman brought her friend into everything burned a hole through Evangeline's heart. "Things change."

"How are you feeling? Are you painting again?"

Evangeline held up her hand. "Still healing."

"And your mother? How is she?"

"Grieving."

The word was said so sadly that Miss Pearson

frowned, her attention shifting from a regular checkup to a deeper introspection. "Grieving? And how does that affect you? How is your relationship?"

Relationship. Evangeline nearly scoffed at the word. This was a question answered many times before to so many people who needed — or thought they needed — to know how the Frost family was getting along after the accident. "She's grieving. She lost her husband. Life is different now."

"She lost her husband, but not her daughter," Miss Pearson replied, trying to read between the lines. She could see the discomfort spread across the teenager's face. "Are things all right between you?" The silence between them answered the school counselor's question. "Would you like to talk about it?"

"Talk about what?" Evangeline asked, hands tightening on the armrests. Pain shot up the back of her right hand and into her wrist at the grip. Despite her rigid posture, her words were calm, almost bored. "That I stole her husband from her? That I ruined the dream? That I can't make up for what I've done?"

Six months she had been meeting with the girl — even before Evangeline's senior year officially started, to prepare her for what was to come and ensure she passed her junior year — but not once had Miss Pearson heard such a confession, one that revealed the fragility of a girl trying so hard to be strong. It brought forth an ache in her heart, a pain for the teenager who was struggling to heal both physically and emotionally while believing, deep down, that she wasn't worthy of it.

"Evangeline, it wasn't your fault."

She cocked her head to the side, a sarcastic smile

playing at the corner of her lips. "They say otherwise."

"Who are *they*?"

"The police. The reporters. The people who write your checks."

Miss Pearson knew the rumors, the speculation of what happened the day of the accident. But she also knew Evangeline, knew she was a good kid with a good heart. "It wasn't your fault," she repeated.

"Why do you keep saying that?"

"Because it's the truth."

"What does anyone know of the truth? They weren't there."

"But you were. So tell me, how did it happen?"

Her eyes stared straight ahead, unwavering, tearless. But her mind, that took her back to the day she tried so hard to forget.

"What's next?" she asked, eyes trained on the road before them.

"Changing lanes, little elf," her father answered. "The road is yours to command! The High Queen of Florida!"

She laughed at that, rolling her eyes at his display of grandeur. Always outgoing, never dull, her father could make even the grumpiest of men and women roll with laughter. But she admired that about him, his openness and friendliness, as well as his ability to recognize the seriousness of any situation.

"Don't forget your blinker. Check your blind spots. Good. See, piece of cake."

"Yeah, you owe me some."

"You don't even like cake."

"No, but I like presents."

He laughed, a rich sound that filled the car. "Yeah, yeah. Keep your eyes on the road, princess."

Evangeline smiled. She'd forgotten about that exchange. She'd forgotten a lot about that day — except the part that came after.

No, she reprimanded herself internally, refusing to let her thoughts stray to that single moment when she knew, irrevocably, that her life had just been shattered to pieces.

Her attention returned to the counselor, who was peering at her curiously. The softness of her eyes, the gentle smile, the way her hands were clasped beneath her chin — Evangeline knew the look well.

And hated every part of it.

"I'm going home," she announced, and left the office before Miss Pearson could protest.

THE SOUNDS OF melodic tunes and silverware clinking against champagne glasses brought forth a sigh when Evangeline returned home, knowing that could only mean one thing — her mother was lost on memory lane.

A beautiful day, everyone said. A moment of true love that was as evident as the sun that shone down on them. High school sweethearts destined for each other from the very beginning.

A wedding that was still talked about fondly, an elegant affair that celebrated the union of two kindred souls, vibrant and happy, the future theirs for the taking.

A marriage that ended too soon, lost now save for the memories on a disk tucked away on a living room shelf.

She heard her father speaking to whoever was holding the camera — her grandfather? The sound of that familiar voice made her smile and follow the path his words created into the living room.

But it wasn't her father she found upon entering.

"Mom!" The sight of her mother crumpled at the base of the couch brought forth a panic that gripped Evangeline's stomach, and she rushed to her side. "Mom, wake up." She smelled the alcohol, saw the overturned bottle spilling onto the carpet. Red wine soaked into the floor, the color dark and ominous.

Blood. So much blood.

Tears welled at the fear of what was unfolding before her.

Another unconscious parent.

Her mother collapsed across her lap.

Death in her hands.

"*Mom*!"

At the rough shake of her shoulders, Edith stirred, though she didn't hear her daughter's gasp of relief. "What are you doing?" she asked groggily, pushing herself away clumsily.

Evangeline helped her to the couch, surprised by how clear her mother's words sounded, how balanced she sat after being propped up by a couple of pillows. "You—you were passed out on the floor. I was scared. I thought—"

"No … Not all of us are so lucky."

The girl recoiled a bit, casting a look over at the wedding video that was still playing. Her mother and father danced on the screen, their first dance, sharing an expression filled with so much love and hope that Evangeline's heart nearly broke all over again. A sob caught in her throat and she pushed it back despite the tears building in her eyes. "Look, Mom, I'm sorry. I was just scared, is all. I saw you there and just panicked, I guess. I'll go make dinner."

"I'm not hungry. I don't need you taking care of me."

"I just want to make something to eat. You don't have to eat with me." Evangeline crossed her arms, hugging herself tightly. A snarky response was on the tip of her tongue, but she bit it back, remembering her promise to be good, to make her mother love her again. It was a vow she was struggling to keep.

"Can I get you anything at all? Mom?" When Edith ignored her and simply watched the television, something close to anger spilled out of her daughter. "Mom, look at me! Say something!"

Again she was ignored, her mother lifting her head a little higher and pressing her lips together tightly. Evangeline's promise to be the good daughter again ripped apart inside her chest. "I don't know what else I can do except tell you a thousand times over and over again that I'm *sorry*! I want you to love me again, and be with me again. Scream at me, hit me, do *something* to let me know you still *feel*!"

Her outburst drained her, left her breathing heavily, tears in her eyes. She'd never once asked her mother for such a display of emotion, but she needed it now. She needed it for herself, for their relationship.

If her mother considered her words at all, she showed

no recognition. Instead she simply turned her eyes to her daughter for the briefest of moments and answered, "I wish it had been you, not him."

SLIPAWAY

SOMETHING HAD BROKEN inside Evangeline, a painful physical break of her soul. Taking over the broken bits was emptiness, an overwhelming sense of nothing that threatened to swallow her whole.

I wish it had been you, not him.

She sat huddled in the corner of her room, wedged between her dresser and closet. Words she'd never thought would pass her mother's lips ate at her, silenced her, condemned her. Fate had taken away her father, hate had destroyed her. A never-ending cycle of forgotten hope, turned heads, downcast eyes, forgiveness never to be had.

I wish it had been you, not him.

She'd tried to overcome the darkness, a kind of depression she'd always heard about but never really believed in. She'd tried to be good, to heal herself and her family. Now her eyes were blank, a locked gaze on a bare wall in a loveless home. Old wounds ached, reminding her of the day the darkness reigned. Silence permeated the air — a void of forgotten affections that could never again be filled.

I wish it had been you, not him.

Her eyes traveled over the paintings that hung on the walls, artwork that had once made her mother so proud. Mixes of glorious color, brushstrokes that created beautiful waterfall landscapes and detailed portraits, canvases that showcased the talent of a rising star in the art community. A family piece, mother and father and daughter at the beach, arms wrapped around one another, the ocean swelling behind him, sunlight wrapping them in a golden aura.

I wish it had been you, not him.

The bite of pain when metal sliced skin. The bitter copper scent that called for death. The warm flow of crimson ribbons against a still-healing leg. A deep vertical wound not to be quelled by fear, foretelling a welcomed end to an unwelcomed life.

I wish it had been you, not him.

It was easy, so easy, to give in, to slip away from this world and into the one her father had left her for. It was hard, too hard, to make up for the past and rise above the obstacles set before her. To sleep, to make it all go away, to leave behind the ones who didn't want her anyway — this was the only path left for her.

"Stay strong, little elf. Stay strong for me."

Her eyes opened at the voice that spoke in her mind. A familiar voice, strong and certain despite the growing fear of a man who knew his time had come. She saw him all over again in that moment before it ended — the moment no one knew about except the two who were there — and heard again the last words he would ever say to her.

Panic overwhelmed acceptance. Evangeline stirred, but her energy had waned with the flow of blood pooled around her. Regret pushed her forward, grasping for the phone on the floor at her feet. A promise made six months ago had her dialing three simple numbers.

She slumped to the floor before the first ring ended, never making contact with the one she sought.

THERE WERE NO kindnesses extended to her this time, no compassion for the girl who took the coward's way out. The fluorescent lights and sterile air mocked her as she recovered, haunted her dreams until, finally, she was well enough to meet with the woman who would decide her fate.

Except this time it wasn't a woman. It was a man, a different adult sent to speak to the troubled teenager who tried to take her own life. *Perhaps the other one gave up,* Evangeline mused as she sat perfectly still in the bed, not sparing the stranger a glance. She'd met with the woman, whose name she couldn't be bothered to remember, twice a day for the past four days. She was tired of the condescension in the older woman's voice, the questions that sounded more like accusations, the annoying click of the pen cap as she spoke.

This man, though, seemed different. Out of the corner of her eye, Evangeline watched him shuffle his papers and adjust his tie as though nervous, then take a seat next to her bed. She hadn't been allowed to leave the psych ward of the hospital since the incident no one but the shrinks wanted to talk about — not that she cared. She was content to stay in the cold, unfeeling room for as long as they would let her. Going home wasn't an option.

She had no home.

"Good morning, Evangeline," the man said, his voice soothing and warm, and surprisingly deep considering his short and lanky frame. "My name is Rick Banshaw. Feel free to call me Rick." He held out a hand in greeting, then dropped it when she flinched, clearly not wanting to be touched. Or perhaps, he considered, the one she sought physical comfort from was the one person who refused to offer it.

"I'm not a psychiatrist, if that's what you're wondering. I'm a caseworker for the Department of Children and Families. Social Services may be a term you're familiar with."

He waited another moment for any kind of response, but the girl before him remained motionless, hands in her lap. His eyes trailed down slender arms to those hands, to the wrist that was still bandaged. The amount of bandages, and how high up they went her wrist and forearm, concerned him. "What do you regret more, the fact that you tried to commit suicide, or the fact that you lived?"

The question startled Evangeline, enough that she turned her gaze to meet his. Indignation, annoyance, and curiosity filled her eyes. She'd expected him to be smirking and was surprised to see the genuine interest in his expression. "Does it matter?"

"I think it does."

32

"Then there's your answer."

Rick smiled softly, settling back in the uncomfortable chair. "Not quite, though I do have a theory." He took her silence as permission enough to continue. "You were in a terrible accident, one that still haunts you. You healed physically from that accident, though you still grieved for your father. But you were doing better, according to your teachers. You were going to school, trying to get back to a normal routine. Then something happened. What, I don't know, but it pushed you over the edge. But you didn't fall, only tripped. You caught yourself and you called for help — you saved yourself. I have to wonder what pushed you in the first place."

She didn't answer, but he hadn't expected her to. Still, he suspected he knew the answer. He'd read the police report — the girl found bleeding to death in a dark and cold bedroom, her mother watching television in the living room with a glass of wine in hand, oblivious to what was happening down the hall. She'd shown little concern for the paramedics' visit, police had said, though after, when giving a statement, reality seemed to settle in and sent her to the bathroom, where she was violently ill. Rick had also noted the comment about that illness, the policeman wondering if it had been the alcohol or the situation that sickened the otherwise ambivalent woman.

Something had transpired between mother and daughter that night, but what, no one knew. Questions had been asked, but neither of them was talking. Rick was brought in, not to get that final answer, but to determine the best solution for the girl. Evangeline's first psychiatrist had given up after only a few days, claiming the attitude of both the girl and her mother were not conducive to effective treatment. Though Rick had to wonder why the hospital bothered to staff a woman who wasn't willing to dig deeper, he was eager still to help the girl in need.

"I want to help you, Evangeline. Tell me what you want, what you need."

What she wanted, she couldn't have. What she needed, her mother had ripped away with her final declaration.

Rick suppressed a sigh, bothered more by the fact that he couldn't read the teenager's mind than her silence. "I invited your mother to join us today." He noted how quickly that got her attention, the change in her breath, the way her eyes narrowed. "I thought that perhaps together we can find out what will help you heal, both mentally and emotionally."

When the girl merely lifted a shoulder, Rick sat up a little straighter and folded his hands in his lap. "Evangeline, do you know what the Baker Act is?"

She rolled her eyes in his direction as an answer. Yes, she knew. She knew she'd been Baker Acted for attempting suicide. She knew she couldn't leave the hospital until the doctors deemed her mentally stable. She knew Social Services had gotten involved. She knew her mother resented her even more as a result.

As if on cue with her daughter's thoughts, Edith walked into her hospital room, only the second time she'd visited. Evangeline sneered internally. She didn't acknowledge her mother. She could be cold, too.

Unfeeling.

Unforgiving.

Merciless.

"Welcome, Mrs. Frost," Rick greeted, gesturing for Edith to take a seat in the chair next to him. "Thank you for coming in today."

"What is this about?" she asked.

Rick could sense the nerves in her jittery voice, in the way her eyes darted around the room — everywhere but at Evangeline. It felt as though the woman was afraid something about her would be revealed.

"To discuss Evangeline and her health," he answered smoothly.

"I already told the doctors, do what you need to do."

Evangeline rolled her eyes, her gaze landing on the television. A game show was on and she feigned interest in the contestant currently guessing the correct prices. Rick noted the movement out of the corner of his eye, but didn't comment on it. Instead, he focused on Edith's answer.

"There are many options to take, Mrs. Frost. This isn't a matter of doing what needs to be done, but rather deciding together what is best for Evangeline. I started to explain just before you came in about the Baker Act. As you both know, Evangeline has been in the psychiatric ward for a few days now and has been evaluated daily. My job isn't to finish the evaluation but to help with what comes next. I am going to meet with you separately and together, and keep track of your progress after the hospital. I'm curious, Mrs. Frost, what you feel would be best for your daughter."

Edith released a sigh, one that was mixed with frustration and boredom. Her fingers tapped on the armrests of her chair, calculating. She didn't notice the way Evangeline's head turned slightly, making it clear that she was listening while pretending not to. Rick, however, saw all that and more.

"A boarding school is fine. One that teaches responsibility and accountability."

Rick held in a sigh of his own. "Boarding schools are often set up for education purposes only, or to address specific behavioral problems. They aren't designed to provide for any kind of emotional or psychiatric counseling. They are also costly."

"Her father set up a college fund when she was born. You can use that money."

Evangeline's brows raised at that, though her eyes remained on the television. Rick stole a glance at the teenager to see her eyes water just a bit. "Mrs. Frost, I don't think you quite understand what—"

"I understand, Mr. Banshaw. I think you just don't understand the real problem."

"Which is what?"

"What she did, and what she should be held accountable for."

There were several layers to that response, none of which Rick wanted to peel back in front of the fragile teenager who lay before him. Frustrated, he took a moment to collect his thoughts and let his gaze wander around the room. There were very few adornments outside of standard hospital décor, and the lack of personality in the room bothered him. There should be pieces of the girl's life all around them, mementos that inspired her to get healthy, be happy. Finally, his eyes landed on a stuffed giraffe next to a vase of orange flowers. "Who are those from?"

Evangeline followed his gaze. "A friend," she replied absently. "He came to see me yesterday."

"Why did he bring a giraffe?"

"Because I like them."

"Why giraffes?"

"I like all animals." She shrugged, her voice stronger at the change of subject. "I used to want to be a vet, but I don't like seeing animals hurting so I changed my mind."

"Do you ever go to the zoo?"

"All the time. Usually by myself since most people don't like it as much as I do."

Rick nodded, his mind reeling. The new information was almost too perfect and gave him cause for excitement. He rose and excused himself, exiting the small room and leaving the two alone. Neither looked at the other, instead focusing their attention on the muted television in the corner. Tension built with each breath, unspoken words cementing a wall between mother and daughter.

Just when Evangeline thought she would leap from the bed and tear that wall down to escape her mother's bored gaze, Rick reentered, cell phone in hand.

"Sorry about that, I had to make a call." He took his seat again, excitement clear in his voice. "I was hoping I would have the opportunity to offer this, but I needed to be sure it would interest you first. Evangeline, what would you say to getting out of here for a bit, joining a program designed to help teenagers who have experienced trauma and hardship?"

"I'm not going to a looney bin."

"It's not a looney bin," Rick chuckled. "It's actually a rather fantastic program out in California. It's relatively established, since it was started almost ten years ago, but somewhat exclusive. They only accept one person a year due to the nature of the program, and they haven't yet selected a candidate for this year. It would give you a chance to get away from the surroundings that are preventing you from healing, while still ensuring you receive proper schooling and counseling. And, perhaps I should mention," he added, watching her carefully, "that it takes place at an animal rehabilitation center."

SAY GOOD-BYE

HE WORKED THE details out with his cousin, who led the Second Hides Program at Kindred Hides Wildlife Preserve. Rick hadn't had the opportunity to utilize the program with any of his cases before, and was eager to introduce Evangeline. He knew she needed the escape, something to get her past her troubles and find light in her life again. The girl seemed excited about the chance to get away, or as excited as she would allow herself to appear.

The only obstacle left to overcome now sat in front of him.

"Edith," he said patiently, trying to keep his voice light. He had brought the woman back to her home, hoping the familiar surroundings would make Edith a little more compliant, and so they could discuss the finer details of the program without upsetting Evangeline. The girl hid it well, but Rick had been working with troubled teens for almost twenty years now and knew all the signs of a teenager doing her best to hide a hurting heart. "Evangeline is only sixteen. Almost seventeen, sure, but not yet. I need your signature and permission to let her do this." He'd explained the program, the rules, everything she needed to know as a mother. And still, she gave him that same disinterested glare. Rick guessed it would be harder to meet with the mother rather than daughter during his time with the family. "It's either this, or she's shipped off to some psych ward that will break her of every ounce of strength she has left. This is something you need to do for her, and for you."

"Why should I?" Edith answered, the slightest of slurs in her words. "She doesn't deserve a second chance. She took someone away from me, all because she's an irresponsible child. After what she's done …"

He struggled to keep his temper in check. Anger would not win here, only gentle persuasion. So he would pretend to be on her side, appeal to the need for vengeance. "Then this program is what she needs. The couple who runs it has gone through several certification classes in childhood development and counseling in order to offer the program. They have volunteered more than one hundred hours each at various children's organizations and are recognized by the state for what they're doing. The Second Hides Program is designed to change behaviors. It targets behavior that doesn't fit within a well-respected society, breaks it, and reshapes it into respect and discipline. The owners of the preserve put the kids to work, hard manual labor every single day. Cleaning out stalls, preparing food, shoveling manure. It's not a vacation. It's a reminder of what happens when you're not responsible."

Though what he was saying was essentially true, albeit with some amount of twisted persuasion, Rick nonetheless lost a little respect for himself for stooping to the woman's level. That self-directed disgust only deepened when he saw Edith's brows lift, as though she were pleased by the thought of putting her daughter to work.

Taking advantage of the moment, Rick held out a pen, that single beacon of hope, the most powerful tool he had at his disposal. "Sign the papers for her release and participation, and let us help her."

EVANGELINE STEPPED OUT of the airport, orphaned in a strange, unknown world. Over her shoulder was an old, frayed backpack that held what few possessions she held dear: a framed photograph of her and her father on a family vacation, a few books she'd read dozens of times, a bundle of art brushes and pieces of canvas, and, her latest acquisition, the stuffed giraffe from her childhood friend.

It still surprised her that he'd come to see her in the hospital, his eyes rimmed in red. In some strange, dark way, her attempt to take her own life had brought them back together, Cam no longer letting her drift away, Evangeline no longer turning away when he looked in her direction. Their friendship was still strained, but repairing itself, sparked by his hospital visit and even more so by his words.

"*We gotta get ya well,*" he'd said, his voice tinted

41

with a southern accent that matched his tousled blonde hair and mischievous green eyes. *"It ain't the same without ya around. I need ya back, Evie."*

She'd almost smiled at the old nickname — almost. Nearly smiled again when Cam handed her the stuffed giraffe and reminded her of their childhood trips to the zoo. Came close to tears when his voice changed then to something close to affectionate.

"I know thing's been rough, Evie, but ya gotta snap out of it. This ain't healthy." He gestured to her bandaged wrist, eyes lingering as his mouth twisted into a frown. *"Maybe I don't know the whole story and maybe I don't wanna know, but it ain't right. I hope you can figure it all out."*

He didn't know the whole story. No one did. No one ever would.

"Evie, look. I know I already said it, but ... I'm sorry. I know you said to forget it, keep my mouth shut, but—"

"I said drop it, Cam," she'd cut in, not allowing him to voice the words she'd already forbidden him to say. She wouldn't, couldn't, speak of that day, and especially not of the secret held between them.

He'd only sighed and shook his head. *"Evie, if I hadn't of—"*

"Cam, either shut up or get out."

He'd surprised her with a gentle kiss to her forehead in response to her harsh reply. Never having seen Cam so sweet before — this was, after all, the boy who was the first to rub mud in her hair and challenge her to dirt bike races — Evangeline wasn't sure how to respond to the gesture. So instead she merely sat there on the bed, keeping her gaze out the window in an attempt to appear indifferent to his friendly affections.

If she tried hard enough, she could still feel his lips warm against her skin. But, she didn't want to try. She didn't want to remember how nice he'd been to that cowardly, damaged girl in the hospital.

"*Jengo the Giraffe will keep ya company. You know, til ya come home.*"

Home. The word felt as foreign to her as the feel of the California sun against her cheeks. She didn't have a home, not anymore. Her mother had signed her away and sent her across the country. Deep down, Evangeline knew she legally still had a mother, but not the way it really mattered.

And, the worst part was, she was starting not to care.

So now she stood outside the airport, having been transported to her flight by Rick, her new caseworker. She'd met with him several times over the past few days, listening intently to his explanations, annoyed that he pried into her family, intrigued by the fact that her mother was so bothered by his examinations into their home life, especially the unannounced visits that were now so frequent. Evangeline knew her mother was embarrassed that the state had gotten involved, but also somewhat enjoyed Edith's discomfort when under Rick's scrutinizing stare.

On some level she supposed she liked the scrawny middle-aged man who asked far too many questions in order to do his job, but had to wonder at his eagerness in shipping her off to a different coast and time zone. He didn't even know her, yet was suspiciously excited about helping her. No one cared that much.

Not about her, anyway.

She couldn't wonder about it too long, though, for

soon she heard a high-pitched voice calling her name from somewhere in the mass of vehicles in the pickup section. Her hazel eyes scanned the crowd lazily, squinting in the bright afternoon sun, taking in the chaos of cars and bodies swarming about. Finally her gaze landed on a sturdy-looking woman with fiery red hair tucked back in a messy bun. The woman, dressed in faded jeans and a flannel shirt, hurried over to her with a wide smile spread across a weather-worn face.

"You must be Evangeline Frost," she stated, her voice coated with a surprising Mid-West accent. "Can't miss a face that pretty! We're so excited to have you! You are going to love Kindred Hides Wildlife Preserve. I'd never leave if I could help it, but someone's gotta do the grocery shopping. Oh! My name's Lettie. Just Lettie, no need for formalities."

The woman named Lettie laughed at the expression on Evangeline's face — the wide eyes glinting with panic, the furrowed brow, the hard-set jaw. "Oh, dear. I get ahead of myself a lot, I'm afraid. Come on, now. We don't want to miss supper! You've never had dinner until you've had a meal on the preserve!"

Evangeline let the older woman drag her down the sidewalk by her elbow, grateful that she didn't try to hug her. The woman seemed like a hugger. She wondered if Rick had warned her against doing so. She'd seen the look on his face when she flinched away from his hand at their first greeting, not one of judgment but rather sympathy — sympathy for the girl who shunned intimacy after being denied it for so long.

Her pondering was cut short when she saw the Jeep Lettie had led her to.

Lettie stopped when she sensed no one was behind her. She turned to see Evangeline a few feet behind her, staring at the vehicle as though expecting it to attack her at any second. The woman regretted having to pick up the teenager in the Jeep, but it was the only vehicle at her disposal that day. Her expression turned sympathetic, her voice surprisingly calm. "Evangeline, sweetie, it's safe. I promise."

She heard the words, but couldn't process them. Evangeline had spent very little time in cars since the accident, and those few instances had been under heavy medication. The pill she'd taken before leaving for the airport had worn off and she wasn't given extra. No, this — the program, the healing — had to be done on her own.

Her hands curled into fists, nails digging into her palms as she forced herself to take a step forward, stomach lurching. Each step made the rock in her gut a little hotter, a little harder, until finally she felt like she'd swallowed liquid fire, but she'd made it. Evangeline sat in the backseat, one hand gripping the door and the other curled around the backpack strap. She sat perfectly straight, eyes forward, buckled in but clearly not comfortable.

Lettie didn't say anything to soothe girl, knowing no words would take away her fear. Instead she just pat her on the back and smiled. "Drive's about two and a half hours. I think you'll enjoy the scenery."

A NEW ESCAPE

SHE DIDN'T ENJOY the scenery, or even remember it.

By the time they arrived at Kindred Hides Wildlife Preserve, Evangeline was exhausted simply from trying not to pass out in panic. Her left palm was bleeding lightly from her fingernails and her stomach ached, though that may have been from hunger, she couldn't tell.

It was dark when the Jeep finally slowed and came to a stop in front of a towering metal gate that reminded the teenager of *Jurassic Park*. Evangeline could only see shadows of the bars from overhead lights before it opened, allowing entry into a woodland escape. For a moment she let her mind wander to an almost humorous place where dinosaurs waited to chase her through the rain before she snapped back to grim attention.

She couldn't see the forests around her but could smell the trees, the dirt, the scent of animals in the distance. In the past, before she lost her life to tragedy, that scent would have excited her, knowing what sights were soon to befall her eyes. Now, she felt only a kind of sad indifference that had her falling back against the seat with a sigh, eyes closed.

She didn't open them again until the Jeep stopped and Lettie turned off the engine. Eager to get out of the vehicle, Evangeline all but leapt from the car before her vision had focused, but when it did, she saw a picturesque cabin nestled between a fencing of grand trees that shadowed the night sky.

The cabin was at least three stories tall, with a beautiful wraparound porch and chimney currently pumping out a thin trail of gray smoke. The place reminded Evangeline of a log cabin, only so much better, with round windows on the first and second floor, a front door made of etched glass, and bright green vines growing up side trellises. The roofing arched down low in the front, creating an overhang that housed wicker furniture and a couple hammocks that swayed gently in the breeze. She imagined the back looked similar.

Surrounding the cabin were shrubs in bloom with pink and white flowers. Oak trees spotted the property, creating shade along the front walk, which was lined with wildflowers. That front walk led to a wide wooden staircase with banisters that looked like thick twisted vines wrapped around driftwood.

"You could stare at it, or come on inside and eat," Lettie teased from the front step. Evangeline dropped her gaze, surprised by the annoyance that instantly bubbled up.

She didn't used to be so quick to anger, but after six months of dealing with her mother's glares — or being ignored altogether — she was finding it harder and harder to suppress any feelings of rage. After all, anger had proven to be the only effective way to get through to her mother. For now, she pushed aside those feelings of ire and forced herself to concentrate on taking one step at a time. That much she could do without lashing out.

"Nah, leave 'em," Lettie said when the girl reached for her bags. "The boys'll get 'em. They like to show off their muscles to all the pretty girls."

She held out a hand to help the teenager up the steps, but Evangeline merely tightened her grip on her backpack straps. Lettie relented and turned, not watching Evangeline's struggle as she hopped up each step while trying to keep her bad knee from buckling. Ignoring the pain and trying hard not to limp, Evangeline followed the older woman inside, reluctantly eager to see what was for dinner based on the smell coming from the kitchen.

The interior of the cabin was just as charmingly rustic as the outside. Each wall reminded Evangeline of driftwood, taking her memories back to weekends and summers spent on the beach back in Florida. The ceilings were high and spotted with lanterns in the shapes of trees or tracks that pointed lights on various wall décor. She saw oil paintings of wildlife, and admired each one that they passed; she saw Western memorabilia hanging on pegs; she saw beautiful quilted blankets hand-stitched by Native American artists, and ran her hand over each one hanging on the wall or over the backs of chairs to see if they were as soft as they looked.

The farther they walked into the cabin, which Lettie

referred to as the "big house" more than once, the homier it felt. Evangeline liked the atmosphere, the warmth, the way she felt safe and tucked away from the world. It was a well-lived-in cabin, a place that invited people to kick off their shoes and relax, and she imaged many a meal was enjoyed within these walls.

The thought of meals made her stomach growl, and she hoped Lettie was taking her to whatever room was letting off that incredible aroma.

"There she is, our newest victim!" a deep voice boomed out from the doorway of a far room. Evangeline jumped at the sudden disturbance in the otherwise quiet air. "Hope you're ready to pick up poop and get manhandled by hungry goats!"

The grin that spread across the man's rugged face almost made her smile. Evangeline suppressed the urge and looked down at the floor, etching his image in her mind: tall and broad shouldered, thick black hair ruffled from the wind, sturdy frame and large hands that suggested years of manual labor, a nose that was almost too large for his face, a well-groomed yet bushy black beard around a grinning mouth, friendly blue eyes.

The eyes — they struck her most of all. Sparkling with a joke yet to be told, staring straight into her without judgment or condemnation. Eyes that made her feel welcome and loved and safe all at the same time.

Her father's eyes.

The realization struck her first — a surge of emotion battling with the shell of indifference she'd tried so hard to build. Then the tears coated her eyes, shaming her enough to keep her attention on the wood floor beneath her feet. She pretended to be fascinated with the woven rug, biting her bottom lip to keep from saying, or doing, something stupid.

If he noticed her discomfort, the man made no mention of it. "You must be starving, gal. The gang's all rounded up for supper, so let's get you settled in. The name's Jett." When she looked up, the smallest hint of interest in her eyes, his grin widened. "On account of my hair," he explained, pointing to his head. "Black as night, they say. Jet black. People been calling me Jett for so long, I've done forgot my real name."

When he winked and gestured for her to join him, Evangeline moved forward, deciding she liked this large mountain man with his large laugh and even larger personality. She knew who he was to her now, a state-appointed guardian assigned to her care until her time in the program was over. Rick described him as a kind of foster parent to watch over her, care for her. Evangeline wondered if he actually would care, or if the money the state gave him for being her temporary legal guardian was what mattered most.

Silently chastising herself for thinking such a bitter thing about a seemingly good man, she followed Jett farther into the house and around a corner toward what she guessed was the kitchen, where she could hear sounds of revelry. The laughter, the joy, was so foreign to her that she needed a moment to recognize what she was hearing before connecting the sound to the grinning faces that turned her way.

So began a flurry of activity that Evangeline couldn't process — a rush of names she couldn't remember, faces that were imprinted in memory, handshakes that stiffened her shoulders, affections she knew could not be felt by people who had known her but minutes.

Pity. That was what she felt from them. An overwhelming, suffocating pity. They knew why she was there, what she had done to herself and others. They knew why she wore the thick bracelet over her left wrist, why she tugged down the edges of her jacket sleeve.

And they pitied her.

She hadn't agreed to the program to be stared at and assessed. She agreed because the only other alternative was being watched in a psych ward. Rick was right, she did love animals. But she wasn't fooled — this was a program for deranged teenagers. They wouldn't let her within ten feet of an animal. But still, she considered as she was introduced to strange face after strange face, at least she wasn't strapped to a bed and forced to take pills every morning.

They sat her in the middle of a long, scarred wooden table decorated with an army's worth of food. Corn on the cob, mashed potatoes, a perfectly cooked and sliced roast, and dishes she didn't even recognize all waited for her. After six months of cooking for herself, and not very healthy or hearty meals at that, the mere thought of so much food overwhelmed her. Many nights she'd gone without dinner, having neither the energy nor the desire to eat alone yet again. Now she would be expected to clean her plate, which worried her only because she wasn't sure she'd be physically able to. The last thing she needed was for one of them to report to Rick that she'd suddenly developed an eating disorder.

After everyone was seated, Jett stood at the head of the table. "Gang, most of y'all have now met the newest member to the preserve, but for those who were too shy to introduce yourself, meet Miss Evangeline Frost." He gestured to the middle of the table. Evangeline attempted a smile and failed, though Jett wasn't deterred. "I trust you'll make her feel like one of the gang in no time."

"We'll get her shoveling goat droppings in no time," Lettie put in at his side, eliciting a chuckle around the table. Only one person didn't share the sentiment, Evangeline noted, glancing at the blonde woman at the other end of the table staring at her through narrowed eyes. In another life, Evangeline might have asked what her problem was, but now she only lowered her gaze and hoped the woman directed her glare elsewhere.

"Now, everyone dig in! Especially you, Evangeline. We gotta put a little meat on them skinny bones!" Jett laughed, as did the others, but Evangeline felt the insult hit deep. Perhaps his words were meant in jest, and she supposed her emotions were a bit fragile, but they still cut through her shell of apathy and brought forth a burning anger.

What did these people know of isolation, surrounded by so many friends and loved ones? What did these strangers understand of hunger, so many nights unfed because of a mother who refused to provide? What did they care if a girl they didn't know took offense to even the simplest of jokes?

But her stomach won over her pride, and she accepted the dishes as they were passed to her. Soon her plate was filled and she occupied herself by eating rather than engaging in the lively conversation around her. A dozen voices became one constant hum as she drowned out the sounds of life around her, her focus solely on filling the aching void inside her, a void that could never be filled with food.

JETT SETTLED BACK in his office chair, ragged and faded with age but comfortable nonetheless. Lettie had been after him to buy a new one for years, but as far as he was concerned, he'd finally broken this one in, let it see him through all the preserve's toughest decisions and most stressful of hardships.

Now he allowed the comfort of that old chair to surround him as he thought about the earlier night, the dinner that he doubted was uncomfortable to anyone except the newcomer. He could sense her fear and annoyance just as easily as he could see the mask of friendliness she tried hard to keep plastered on her face. He'd expected a little bit of an attitude from the teenager. All of the program participants came in with a chip on their shoulder and something to prove.

He wasn't sure what Evangeline felt she had to prove, but the need was there nonetheless. Her first night was spent observing the people she would be working with, and there was no telling what tomorrow would bring. Now that she was fed and settled in her new room, it was time for Jett to check in. He'd put off the call he knew he needed to make, preferring to wait until he had a full assessment of his new charge before calling the caseworker, also known as his younger cousin.

Rick answered on the second ring. "Hey, Jett. I was starting to worry."

"All's good," Jett answered his cousin, rubbing a

hand over his face.

"How is Evangeline?"

"All settled in. This girl, she's certainly different."

"How so?"

"Doesn't talk much, that's for certain. Seems to go back and forth from sad to angry to doesn't give a damn. I can't get a good read on her like I can on the other kids that come through here."

On the other end of the phone, Rick sighed. "She's got up a wall, Jett, that's for sure. No one, not even her friend from childhood, can break through it. And whatever happened to make her attempt suicide just made that wall thicker and higher. Did she get settled in okay?" he asked when Jett returned his sigh with an even deeper one.

Jett waved a hand toward the bunks, which were situated within walking distance behind the main cabin. "Oh, yeah. Lettie gave her the empty room next to one of the keepers, Lana. Lettie says she just sat down on the bed and stared at the wall. Seemed miserable, Lettie said."

"From what her doctors and the school counselor say, she hasn't smiled since it happened, let alone laughed. She needs to find that spark again, Jett. This may be her last chance."

No pressure, huh?" Jett's second sigh was heavy, filled with regret and sadness. "She seems like a good enough kid, I suppose. No history of violence, not one of them hooligans we've brought on before, the kind that would rather spray paint the walls than fill a few feed buckets. The troublemakers are harder to deal with, considering they hate authority and all. We get through to all of them either way, but those types are more difficult. I can handle depressed a lot easier than I can criminal."

"I hope so. I tried to get her to meet up with one of her friends before she left, but she seems to think no one will even realize that she's gone. Maybe being around you and everyone at the preserve will get her talking, help you figure out what she needs."

Jett glanced out the window at the bunks, where almost all of the preserve keepers chose to live. Evangeline's light was still on, and he wondered if she was still staring at the wall. "We'll figure it out, Rick. She's in good hands here."

And so he made a promise to his longtime friend — that he would not fail Evangeline. It was a promise he could only pray she'd let him keep.

WHEN THE SUN RISES

"COME ON, LITTLE elf. Time for your lesson."

"Dad. It's Sunday, the day of rest."

The man laughed, the corners of his blue eyes crinkling as he leaned over and shook his daughter's mattress. "The Frosts never rest! We're always up for adventure! Get ready, we're going driving!"

Begrudgingly, the sixteen-year-old dragged herself out of bed and got ready for the day. It was only a half hour later that she joined her father in their Jeep – this time with her in the driver's seat.

"Hey now, none of that sourpuss face," her father playfully chastised when he glanced over to see her scowling. "It's not that *early. Besides, your birthday is coming up, which means your drivers license test!"*

"Yeah, yeah," Evangeline *grumbled as she started the engine. Her scowl turned to a grin when the radio began blaring the sounds of Queen's* Bohemian Rhapsody. *"Seriously?"*

"Gotta get pumped up for the road!"

"You are such an old man."

But she turned the song up anyway and they pulled out of the driveway, her father head-banging in the seat next to her.

The feel of bright sunlight against her cheeks, the sound of a bird's call over a tractor's engine, the scent of nature and hard work — the room Evangeline woke up in was certainly not her own.

Music sounded in her ears against her will, memories from a dream she didn't want to relive and certainly didn't want to dwell on. Rolling onto her back, staring up at the patterns of sunbeams and shadows on the high wooden ceiling, she recalled the previous night instead.

It had taken hours to fall asleep, kept awake by strange grunts and roars, high-pitched chirps, and other sounds she couldn't identify. None of them frightened her — she'd spent enough time in zoos to guess what noise belonged to what animal or at least make a good guess — but they disrupted her sleep nonetheless. The most noise she ever encountered back home was the occasional car alarm and maybe a siren in the distance. When she finally drifted into an uneasy rest, she dreamed of heartache, a sensation that followed her into her waking hours.

Shaking off the negative thoughts and feelings, Evangeline got out of bed and dressed for the day, not sure about her choice of footwear. She supposed they would tell her what she needed to wear. After dressing, she stepped into the morning light and made the short walk to the main cabin. For a moment, she paused on the back porch, glancing around and thinking that if she tried hard enough, she could pretend she was away on vacation, camping, or perhaps splurging on a cabin resort. The crisp and clear woodland air afforded her that much of a fantasy before Evangeline rolled her eyes at her own foolishness and stepped across the threshold.

"There she is!" Lettie cried when Evangeline entered the kitchen. She stood at the stove, her sturdy frame wrapped in a bright yellow apron that covered worn work pants and a red-flowered shirt. "I was just about to send in one of the gals to rustle you up."

Evangeline sat at the table and stole a quick glance at the clock, surprised to see it was barely eight a.m. She'd gotten used to sleeping until noon almost every day, even on school days.

"Days start early 'round here," Lettie said, grinning when Evangeline merely stifled a yawn. "Gotta get to those animals before they start complaining about a late breakfast! And, believe me, they get to complaining pretty quickly. You won't have to get up as early as some of the others, but you won't get many late mornings in bed either. But I assume Rick covered all that with you."

Evangeline only nodded, briefly thinking back to the conversation with Rick about her new home for the next three to six months — however long it took, he'd told her.

This is your time, Evangeline. The Second Hides Program is meant to help you. It's not a vacation by any means, though. You'll be expected to work, get up early, follow orders, be responsible. But you won't be forced to reveal anything about yourself that you're not comfortable revealing. Second Hides isn't like other programs where you're expected to sit there and talk about your feelings. It's more personal. It lets you heal on your own time, on your own terms, in a place that doesn't remind you of the past."

"Or of *her*," Evangeline muttered, saying what she knew Rick was thinking but would never voice.

"Did you say something, dear?"

Evangeline took in a deep breath, pressing her palms against the table. "Um … Just wondering what you'd like me to do."

Lettie turned back to the stove. "First we'll get some breakfast in you, then you can start the day with Caster."

THIRTY MINUTES LATER, Evangeline left the safety of the main cabin. She ended up changing into old jeans and a long-sleeved T-shirt she didn't mind getting dirty, as instructed, then laced up the boots Jett had given her after breakfast. Once dressed, she barely spared herself a glance in the mirror. She knew what she'd see and wasn't happy with it — dark shadows under her hazel eyes, the long scar along her jaw, gaunt cheeks after so many months of not eating right.

Tying back her hair, Evangeline decided she was as ready as she'd ever be for her first day of work and left the small room behind. It was empty, save for her luggage and what few personal items she brought, an empty room to match what she felt inside her own heart. But, she supposed it would do for her time at the preserve, with its log cabin feel, small window overlooking a large garden, and single bed next to a scarred wooden dresser.

Though it was early, the heat was already rising. But Evangeline was a Floridian through and through, and relished 90-degree temperatures. She basked in the heat as she followed a narrow dirt trail through a small patch of woods. The path was lined on either side by a handmade wood-and-wire fence, though she guessed it was more for aesthetics than keeping animals out, considering the three peacocks on the trail ahead of her.

She couldn't see much of the preserve from the trail, or the cabin for that matter. Her brief stay thus far had yielded her a view of the cabin kitchen, a vegetable garden, and a nature trail. And, so far, she wasn't impressed.

That all changed when she stepped off the trail, and into the Kindred Hides Wildlife Preserve.

Evangeline had been to many zoos in her almost-seventeen years, and to Disney's Animal Kingdom several times, but nothing compared to this. Standing on a hilltop that overlooked most of the preserve, she could see the expanse of land that stretched out in a wide circle that was surrounded by forests on all sides. A dirt-packed trail wound around the enclosures in a spiderweb-type design that arced out from a central manmade pond, allowing access from the front or back of each area.

She could clearly see that every animal — or at least, every species — had its own place to roam, separated by tall fences, wide moats or lakes, and even bridges in some areas. Closest to her was a group of goats, tiny furry bodies crowding around what she guessed was their breakfast. Just beyond them, deer or antelope of some sort, followed by elephants. She wondered if each section was separated by continent, since the animals in her immediate view were from Africa, and beyond that she saw a sign with a picture of a jaguar, which told her South America came next.

People milled around, some dressed in matching dark green shirts and pants, others in flannel. All of them wore thick black boots that she guessed were waterproof, considering how many of them were glistening with water or mud. Several keepers were inside the empty enclosures, cleaning and refilling food buckets or shoveling manure. Another was running a tractor, moving large branches from a tree that must have come down recently. She saw that a fence had been damaged in the process, which explained why that enclosure was empty as well.

"Is there a reason why you're just standing there?"

Evangeline turned, startled to see the grumpy blonde from the previous night standing a few feet away. She hadn't heard anyone approach, though with all the sounds going on around her, supposed that wasn't too much of a stretch.

"Um … I'm supposed to find Caster, to work with him."

"Well you're not going to find him just standing here," the woman, who Evangeline vaguely remembered being introduced as Ash, replied. She gestured down the trail. "He's probably by the goats. Usually starts the morning shoveling out the pen. That's about all you'll be good for, so get to it and don't screw anything up."

"I won't." There was an edge to her response, and Ash caught it.

"Don't get prissy with me," she ordered, slinging a

shovel over her shoulder. "You're only a temp. You don't get the respect everyone else does. Now get to work before I tell Jett it's time for you to go back to whatever slum you came from."

She could have been angry, Evangeline supposed, but instead she chose to roll her eyes and make a mental note to avoid that brat of a woman as much as possible. In a way, she understood the attitude. She was, after all, truly just a temp, an outsider, someone who was given a free ride to a pretty cool place. Unlike the other keepers, she didn't have to earn her position.

"I'll prove you all wrong," she whispered, brushing off the encounter with a firm set of her jaw and pushing negative thoughts away. She wanted to be happy her first morning at the preserve, no matter what.

She wanted to be happy, period. And this place, with its miles of green forest and myriad of animals, called to her in a unique way. With each step she took she immersed herself deeper in its culture, exploring every nook and corner while making her way down the trail and finally stopping at the main entrance. Excitement welled within her as she took in more of the preserve, and she could only hope that they let her be a part of the care-taking process.

10

A PIECE OF PARADISE

"SHE'S A BEAUTY, huh?"

Evangeline jumped, startled by the voice that spoke behind her, annoyed that a second person had snuck up on her in less than ten minutes' time. She turned to see a young man staring back at her with a smirk. He was tall and broad shouldered, toned arms and calloused hands testament to his dedication to hard work. His jeans and shirt were already dirt stained, boots coated in mud, and he had dark smudges on his angled cheekbones that brought out the bright green of his eyes. She couldn't tell how old he was, maybe early twenties.

"The preserve, she's a beauty," he said again, running a hand through dark and damp hair that fell in waves around his ears. He squinted in the morning sun as he stared down at her, eyes crinkling slightly at the corners. His face was roughened with years of weather and hard work, but still looked charmingly youthful. "Always takes newcomers by surprise, seeing it for the first time."

She didn't want to admit to her admiration — of the preserve or of him. Instead she merely shrugged and glanced around as though bored, shading her eyes from the bright morning light with one hand. "I'm supposed to find someone named Caster."

"Well, you found him." The man named Caster lifted a brow when she frowned up at him and he took a moment to observe the new girl. She was pretty in a wounded innocence kind of way, with dark auburn hair that probably hadn't been brushed in a week, hazel eyes that looked disinterested but likely saw any and everything, a wide mouth that he guessed packed one hell of a smile, if she knew how to. The bitter look didn't suit her, and deep down he hoped he'd get to see the other side of her emotional spectrum.

"You're Caster?"

"The one and only." He leaned the shovel he was holding against a fence. "Real name's Lancaster. My parents thought it would be cute to name me after the city I was conceived in. I prefer Caster. Sounds more mysterious." He grinned when she merely huffed. "So you're Evangeline? Got a nickname?"

"No."

"Want one?"

"No."

The second *no* was tinted with an urgency that had him biting back a sarcastic retort. "How old are you?"

"Almost seventeen."

He was amused by the answer, noting that she wanted to appear older than she was. "I just turned twenty-two, myself. Been here since I was seventeen, officially anyway. I've been coming here since I was a kid, did some work as a teen, and ended up staying on. I'm hoping to be part of our expansion in Africa, but that's a totally different story. Bottom line, the preserve is a great place. You won't want to leave either."

She doubted that, but didn't voice her thoughts. "So, what do you want me to do?"

"How about a tour first?" He took her silence as agreement and picked up the shovel. "Alright then, let's start here."

Wordlessly, he started down the hill for the first enclosure. "All of the preserve is kind of wrapped up nicely in a circle, so nothing is tucked away in random corners or anything. Makes it easier to navigate and do our rounds. The big house and bunks, obviously, are up on the hill." He glanced over his shoulder, wondering why she was so far behind him. While he waited for her to catch up, he saw why — she was limping, favoring her right leg, though she tried not to show it. "You need a hand?"

"No."

He rolled his eyes and continued forward, approaching their first stop. Caster held out his arms, gesturing to the empty pen behind him, though they could hear muffled sounds coming from the waist-high stalls that lined the back wall. "Welcome to Station G, commonly known as the goat pen. We currently have twelve African pygmy goats, all either in various stages of rehabilitation or need a place to stay until a space opens for them at their respective zoos. We call those guys our squatters."

He chuckled at his own joke, then took a bag out of his pocket and shook it. A herd of goats ran out from the stalls, twisting around one another and racing for the fence in a flurry of hooves. One of the goats, black all over except for small white patches on his chest and rump, shoved his way to the front. "This here is PJ," Caster said, feeding the goats their morning treats through the fence. "He's pretty bossy and doesn't like very many people. Hell, I don't think he likes anyone at all, now that I think about it. He's been here for a while, got himself kicked out of his last home for head-butting one too many guests."

Evangeline watched the goats eat, yearning to pet them but forcing her hands in her pockets instead. She had to admit, they were adorable, especially the one called PJ. She'd have to find a way to sneak back here and pet them through the fence when no one was looking.

When the last of the treats were gone, Caster shoved the empty bag back in his pocket and gestured for Evangeline to follow. She fell into step behind him, glancing around at each enclosure and building he pointed out.

"Over there, behind the goats, we have our cows and chickens. You can see the top of the barn around the corner. They are here mainly just for us, rather than rehab. We don't slaughter them," he said quickly, noting the look of disgust on her face. "We use them for milk and eggs. Our hamburgers come from the grocery store."

They walked a bit farther down a narrow trail until they came up behind a thick metal and wooden structure. "Here we have the white rhinos. I know, you're probably thinking they look gray, not white. Their name comes from the Dutch word, *wijd*, which actually means 'wide.' As in, these guys have really wide mouths. English-speaking settlers later misinterpreted the word to mean 'white' and ended up calling these guys white rhinos. Black rhinos, on the other hand, have much narrower mouths. Just one of many rhino facts."

"Just a theory," Caster heard the girl mumble after he'd turned around.

Slowly, he faced her again. "What was that?"

She drew in a breath, wondering if she should repeat herself. Something about his cocky stance made her want to prove him wrong. "It's just a theory," she said a little louder this time. "Never proven outside of oral history."

Crossing his arms, Caster leaned against the fence and stared at the girl. "So, you're some kind of rhino specialist?" When she merely lifted a shoulder, he shook his head. "Let's keep going then."

Evangeline glanced through the thick steel bars as they passed, seeing three rhinos sleeping against a wall. They had an entire field complete with a large pond to roam, but she supposed they preferred the shade of their hut in the early-morning heat, even if it was constructed of concrete floors and metal bars. Part of her longed to reach through those bars and touch one of them, never having felt a rhino's hide before.

"Next to the not-really-white rhinos are the elephants." Caster came to a stop at the next enclosure and leaned against a sixteen-foot fence made of thick cables that surrounded a circular field in horizontal rows. There was a large barn at one end of the field that she guessed housed the animals at night, along with a huge metal contraption with a monitor on one side that read numbers she didn't understand. The field itself was full of grass, tires, toys, trees, and everything else she supposed made for an elephant's playground paradise.

"These are all female African elephants," Caster explained, gesturing to the six on the field. "We have two males, but they can't generally be out at the same time as the females. They get a little, shall we say, *friendly*." He winked at her, amused by the expression on her face that told him she thought he was a complete moron. "The males can't generally be out at the same time either. We actually have two enclosures so one of the males can be out by himself, but it's being upgraded right now. A few of the elephants are here for rehabilitation, while others are here for breeding. We actually just had a calf born a few weeks ago. He's still in the barn with the mother, but I'm sure you'll see them soon."

She wished she could have seen them right then and there, but didn't say so. Caster saw that wish in her eyes. "Fun elephant fact," he added to keep her interest. "See how those three females have backed up to Angel, the one in the center? That means they know she's in charge and are showing submission. They've made her the matriarch, essentially. Unless, of course, you want to refute that fact, almighty animal scientist." He shot her a grin, and, when she didn't return it, he gave up and continued the tour.

Evangeline followed Caster as they moved on. As they passed the enclosure, she glanced through the cables to see one of the elephants staring back at her with an expression so humanely curious that she nearly laughed out loud. They held eye contact for a moment longer before Evangeline broke her gaze and looked forward, nearly bumping into Caster, who had stopped when he realized she was no longer behind him.

"You coming?" he asked, his question light and humored. Evangeline nodded and returned her stare to the ground. "The next few sections are various kinds of antelope and deer. Some Eastern Bongos, some bushbucks, a few others. You probably won't work much with them, since they are more of a specialized group for us here at the preserve and have specialists working with them so we can return them to the wild. The extent of my work is delivering food and hauling away waste for compost. But, they are pretty awesome to watch. I'm partial to the bongos, personally. They are the largest of the antelopes and males and females both have horns, which is rare. Plus, they just look really cool."

They headed up a boardwalk separating two pastures. A small lake spanned both enclosures, running beneath the bridge. Evangeline looked over both sides, seeing animals she recognized from trips to the zoo as a kid but didn't know by name. She made a mental note to come back at some point and read about them further.

Everywhere he took her, Evangeline found herself immersed in wonder. Caster was right — the preserve was impressive, and magnificently beautiful. She hadn't expected it to be so large, so nearly intimidating in its size. Animals from all corners of the earth greeted her, some intrigued enough to approach the edges of the fence, others hiding in the shadows of their wooded enclosures. She carefully observed them all, eyeing them as closely as they eyed her, wondering if and when she would have the chance to interact.

Caster watched her as well, noting the subtle changes in her demeanor when they came across an animal she was particularly fond of. The goats, for sure. He wasn't sure why she tried to hide her affections or thoughts, but guessed that her wall would start to come down the longer she was at the preserve, or maybe once they reached the next enclosure if Jett was right about her favorite animal. Hopefully some of her annoyingly standoffish behavior would start to disappear as well.

"The last of the big game for today," he said as they rounded a corner, "are the giraffes." He kept his gaze on her, seeing the interest register in her eyes. Her back straightened ever so slightly and she instantly turned her attention to the enclosure on their left. "We currently have six females and one male, all reticulated giraffes except for one masai. We used to have a few others, but they were recently reintroduced to preserves in Africa."

"How do you tell them apart?"

"The species?"

When the girl nodded, her eyes never leaving the enclosure, Caster shrugged. "I'm not an expert on all of them, but I can pick out the differences. Masai, like Checkers over there," he pointed across the yard to a smaller and younger giraffe, "have more of a leafy pattern and their fur surrounding the markings is darker. Reticulated are square. Nubian are almost spotted. There are nine subspecies total, but like I said, I'm no expert. I'm getting there though. Jett is making me study them in preparation for hopefully taking over in Africa. But for now, we run a successful breeding program with our main stud." He tapped a plaque attached to a wooden post at the front of the gate.

Evangeline read the plaque, which stated simply, *Ruke*. "Roo-key," she pronounced quietly.

"Ruke, rhymes with Fluke," Caster corrected her. "He's the top dog here, so to speak. His offspring are in high demand due to his bloodline. Both his parents were wild, which means a better bloodline compared to a lot of giraffes in captivity. He's pretty temperamental and doesn't like many people, though, so keep your distance."

Unable to help herself, Evangeline moved forward and pressed herself against the fence, hands clasping the metal. She wasn't sure why, but giraffes always held a special place in her heart. She loved everything about them — the way they moved, the way their eyes held a look of such peace, the way they stood so tall and proud.

Her breath hitched when one of them caught sight of the two humans just outside the gate and started walking over. Excitement curled in her stomach and her fingers tightened on the fence, but she stood perfectly still until the graceful female came to a stop mere feet away, looking first at Caster and then at the unfamiliar face.

Evangeline swallowed, eyes never leaving the giraffe. She barely breathed when the female lowered her head and sniffed at her fingers, wet nose tickling her skin. In one slight movement, Evangeline lifted a finger and stroked that nose, then blew out a breath when she was dismissed and the animal returned to its tree to graze.

"Well, maybe I oughta call you the giraffe whisperer," Caster put in with a grin. "That's Lady Regal, Lady for short. She isn't usually so curious." He stepped closer to Evangeline when she shifted to get a closer look, and as she did, the edge of her left sleeve slid down. Not much, but enough for him to see the top of a scar hiding beneath a thick bracelet.

He knew what she'd done; or, rather, what she'd tried to do. They all did — after all, that was the entire point of the program. But to see the reason in person, even if only one small part of it, still caught him off-guard.

"Um … Well, that about concludes the tour. How about we get back to the goats? We will start the day there."

He held out a hand, but Evangeline ignored the gesture. Instead they walked back to the goat pen with the newcomer a few feet behind the veteran, both with their hands in their pockets.

A DAYS HARD WORK

EVANGELINE FLOPPED DOWN on her bed face first, utterly exhausted. She hadn't even changed out of her work clothes, save for the boots she'd kicked off at the door. Muscles burned, an aching testament to a full day of manual labor. Limbs were limp, a reminder that she was never one much for exercise. Her mind was blank, unable to form a coherent thought other than how completely tired she was. At some point she'd have to get up and drag herself in for dinner, but right now, she was perfectly content to lay there and feel sorry for herself.

In the cabin only a short distance from the bunks, Lettie put the finishing touches on dinner. The scent of tuna ranch casserole topped with breadcrumbs — a favorite among their group — wafted throughout the cabin, drawing in keepers and workers from all corners of the preserve.

"Where's the greenhorn?" Jett asked with a wide grin as he took a seat, running a hand through freshly washed hair.

"Probably out *not* helping with the daily chores," Ash, the resident large mammal specialist, put in from the end of the table. She flipped her braid over her shoulder, observing her nails.

"I saw her go into the bunk just a few minutes ago," Tatiana, one of the keepers and plant specialists, replied before Jett could answer Ash, who was known for saying things just to rile people up. "She looked pretty beat."

Caster swallowed a mouthful of tuna casserole. "I worked her good," he boasted with a grin. "She's probably out like a light."

"How did she do today?"

"Pretty good for a newb," Caster answered Jett around another mouthful of pasta. "Didn't say much and was kind of, shall we say, *testy*, but followed orders like a champ. I caught her petting the goats a few times when she was supposed to be shoveling out the gravel, but she snapped to it pretty quickly."

Jett nodded, pleased with the report. He'd checked in a few times throughout the day, seeing Evangeline hard at work in the goat pens, and hoped that she'd worked enough to take her mind off of certain other things. That was part of the program — distraction. If the kid was too busy to think about anything other than the task at hand, then said kid wouldn't be doing anything wrong. Or, in Evangeline's case, anything self-harming.

He glanced over at Lettie, who nodded back. "How

about you take our greenhorn a plate? I think we can excuse her from the table for one night."

Lettie did as directed, filling a large plate and stepping outside, into the growing dusk. As she walked, she listened, loving the sounds of night at the preserve. It was here, just outside the cabin she'd help build with her own two hands, that she felt most at peace.

Kindred Hides started as a dream for one young couple hopelessly in love, searching for their path in life, and without a penny to their name. Lettie met Jett when they were both teenagers — he at fifteen and she at fourteen. Times had been different then, couples marrying younger, and so they were wed just after Lettie's seventeenth birthday. They'd hoped to start a large family right away, but fate had other ideas.

Instead, they took to traveling, living out of their RV from state to state until their trip that started in Missouri and detoured to the Dakotas ended in California. By then, they'd seen enough of the country to want to settle down, discover their purpose in life.

It had always been Jett's dream to help save the environment, and Lettie's to save animals. Once, in another life, as Jett liked to say, he'd planned on helping children, and even earned various childhood development certifications to care for the younglings. But then the natural world called to him, just as Lettie did, and his path changed again. They'd been called all types of tree-hugger and hippy names over the years, and embraced every one of them. Because from those names and from those dreams was born Kindred Hides Wildlife Preserve.

Everyone said it couldn't be done, that two kids with nothing to their name except a battered RV could never start up a preserve, let alone afford to keep it running. But they worked hard, all day every day at any job they could get until they'd scraped together enough money to purchase the property. Staying focused on their goal meant not allowing themselves any luxuries in life, but they didn't need luxuries. They only needed their dream.

Getting permits and licenses proved more difficult, as it meant making sure their starting enclosures and structures were built to code and that they were financially capable of supporting whatever animals came to stay with them. Donations helped, as did partnering with the city and securing several other contracts with wildlife programs that believed in their cause — rehabilitation and reintegration into the wild.

Their first animal had been a grizzly bear whose only options were captivity or death after terrorizing a small town in southern Montana. Next came a pair of mountain lion cubs abandoned by their mother in the wild. And after that came two of their own kids, fate seeming to favor them for once — until it took one away.

Building their preserve and their life around it took time, and a lot of backbreaking hours in the hot California sun, but with each new animal came more respect from the community until, finally, they were able to say they were officially living the dream. They still dreamed big and made plans for their preserve, still smiled and nodded politely when others continued to call their goals mere pipe dreams. Even their Second Hides Program was scoffed at in the beginning, naysayers refusing to believe that animals and hard work could change the attitudes of troubled teens. But no matter what anyone said, Jett and Lettie knew they'd get it all done together.

Shaking herself from her memories, Lettie continued the short trip to the bunks and knocked lightly on Evangeline's door. She didn't get an answer, but entered anyway, biting back a chuckle when she saw the girl splayed out across the bed, one arm hanging over the edge.

"First day'll get ya," Lettie said when Evangeline stirred, pushing herself up to a sitting position.

"I'll be better tomorrow."

Lettie noted the defensive tone. "Ah, you work at your own pace. This ain't a prison. Would prison have food this good? Tuna ranch casserole," she said as she handed the tray over. Evangeline accepted the food and reached for the drink, then recoiled and quickly pulled down her sleeve when the edge rode up.

"Do you want to talk about it?" Lettie asked softly, hating to see the look of such despair spread across the girl's face. She pressed her lips together when Evangeline bristled ever so slightly.

"Rick said I wouldn't have to talk."

"You don't, dear," Lettie answered quietly, feeling as though she'd crossed a line somewhere. "But if you ever need to, we're all pretty good listeners."

Evangeline waited until Lettie left before all but attacking the plate of food. The casserole was gone in minutes, washed down by ice-cold water. She contemplated returning the plate to the kitchen, but knew questions would be asked of her dinner disappearance, so instead she set the tray down on the floor and stripped off her filthy clothes. She could have showered, washed away the dirt and grime of the day, but her body told her to stay in bed. Every part of her ached and encouraged her to lay perfectly still until sleep could find her.

She knew what they were doing, why Caster had forced such hard labor on her all day long. Work her every minute of the day, no breaks between shoveling and hauling and feeding. Never taking a moment to stop and reflect on the moment, always keeping pace with the demands of the animals. Make sure her mind stayed focused on the task at hand, not talking about anything except the preserve. It was all a ploy to take her thoughts off everything else, off the past, off what she'd done to herself, off the reason why she was there in the first place.

And it worked. As much as she hated to admit it, Caster's tough and unrelenting push for hard labor kept her focused. She didn't think about her father, her mother, about Cam and school, about any of it. She saw only the animals, heard only their range of sounds.

Until now.

In the quiet of her bunk, only steps away from total strangers who knew nothing about her life but likely judged her all the same, Evangeline felt those thoughts taking hold once more. Loneliness settled in, reminding her that she had no one left to turn to, no one who could truly understand what it felt like to live with such guilt.

She didn't deserve redemption. She wasn't worthy of sitting at a table full of good people. She'd taken a life, and wasn't strong enough to live her own.

With those thoughts racing through her mind, Evangeline fell into a deep, fitful sleep.

AN INTRODUCTION

SHE SPENT HER first week at Kindred Hides Wildlife Preserve mired in the ways of the land. Days passed in the midst of goats and deer, relatively harmless animals that taught her basic care techniques. Nights became lessons in education, a tutor visiting after dinner to coach the girl who could barely keep her eyes open. But still she learned and completed assignments, in hopes of at least earning her high school diploma in the future.

She owed her father that much.

It was on the eighth day that her life at the preserve changed. Evangeline stood on the edge of the goat enclosure, watching as the small, furry bodies huddled around buckets of hay. A laugh almost escaped when one of the goats, the ornery creature named PJ, crawled into the bucket and plopped down, effectively blocking the others from eating.

"He does that a lot," Caster said as he approached, shovel in hand. His face was streaked with dirt, hair damp with sweat. "He's a bit of a jerk."

Evangeline shrugged and got back to work, picking up a metal bucket by the handle with her right hand. As she pulled upward, a cramp in her fingers had her gritting her teeth in pain and dropping the bucket. Pellets spilled out, the sound calling over the herd of goats.

Hooves surrounded her, stepping on her feet and kicking at her shins as the goats hustled for the pellets. Their nimble mouths scooped up what would normally be their daily treats in small handfuls now offered by the bucketful. Before she could attempt to clean any of it up, Caster was at her side, pulling her out of the herd before they could bruise her more than they already had.

"I'm sorry," she said, her voice laced with tears. "I'll clean it up."

"Don't worry about it. So they get some extra treats, no biggie," Caster replied. He took her right hand in his own. "Did you hurt yourself?"

Evangeline tried to pull her hand away, but his grip held firm. She didn't like being touched. It reminded her too much of her time in physical therapy, being poked and prodded to see what still hurt and what would always hurt. Reminded her of the fact that she had caused her own pain.

"No. Just … an old injury … from the accident." It nearly hurt to admit where the injury came from, but she felt like she needed to tell him, needed him to understand that she hadn't meant to drop the bucket.

Caster observed her hand. From the outside, it looked

perfectly normal, though her fingers were a bit bony. "I'm a master at hand massages," he told her. "I learned with Lettie, since she's got arthritis. You ever need one, you just let me know." He waited until Evangeline nodded, then gestured with his head. "Come on, I want to show you something."

She let him lead her, excitement building the closer they got to the giraffes. They hadn't let her come back to this part of the preserve since her initial tour, though she'd been secretly hoping to visit again.

Instead of stopping at the front gate, Caster led her around the field to the barn at the back. Evangeline craned her neck, taking in the massive structure, with its metal support beams, wooden dividers, and hay-coated flooring in each large stall.

"When it's cold out or we're having really bad weather, or we have to do something medical, we bring the giraffes in here," Caster informed her. "They also come in at night, just for safety purposes. Most of the time we let them roam the field, let them live in a more natural state, but sometimes we have to bring them in during the day. And, sometimes they just don't want to go out."

Evangeline followed him, taking in each sight. There were several individual stalls, all of them wide set with feeders and water dispensers. Heavy doors latched in front of each one. In front of the stalls was a walkway that fit perhaps four people side by side. At the end was a table with various tools and items she couldn't identify or even begin to guess what they were used for. Bales of hay were stacked in the far corner, next to a whiteboard with what she figured was a feeding schedule.

Her breath hitched when they stopped in front of a

closed stall. On the outside the nameplate read *Ruke*. Between the bars of the door she could see the prized male giraffe, clearly not happy at being interrupted from his afternoon nap.

"He's been acting a bit strange lately, so the vet is coming in today to check him out. We kept him in here today since he can be a pain in the ass to get back inside when he knows he's supposed to. Not that he's been going outside a whole lot anyway. He's been kind of depressed." Caster started up a set of metal stairs that led to the top of the stall. "But I figured since he was in here, maybe you'd like to meet him."

Evangeline hurried up the stairs, not even bothered by Caster's chuckle or by the slight throbbing in her knee. She stopped at his side, peering into the stall. She was about waist high with the top railing, putting her nearly eye level with Ruke.

"Ruke here is seventeen feet tall. Not the tallest a giraffe can be, but still impressive. The horns on his head are called ossicones. Kind of like horns but not really, since they are actually covered with fur and skin. They are made of ossified cartilage, like our ears. Well, kind of, I guess. Anyway, when giraffes are born, the ossicones are flatter against the head and grow as they get older. Watch out for them. Ruke likes to head-butt people and send those ossicones directly into your forehead, or sometimes your shoulder. I've got the bruise to prove it." Caster grinned over at her.

"Anyway, he may be a brat, but he's beautiful. And he knows it." Caster handed Evangeline a small branch. "Acacia leaves. His favorite treat, aside from Romaine lettuce. See for yourself."

Evangeline took the treat, noting the way Ruke's leaf-shaped ears perked up. She watched him carefully, her eyes never leaving his, holding her breath as he turned and approached the railing. She held out the food as an offering, her expression neutral. She'd fed plenty of giraffes before at other zoos, but never this close, at this level, with someone who was actively encouraging her to bond with the animal.

A long, purple tongue wrapped around the leaves, tugging them from her hand. Evangeline released her breath as the foliage was pulled from her fingers. Her hand now free, she kept it extended and Ruke moved forward, his wet nose sniffing for more. Even at her empty hand he stayed, large chocolate eyes peering into hers. In those eyes Evangeline saw what her future could be, what *she* could be — just as peaceful, just as content to simply *be*.

A small smile formed when Ruke allowed her to lower her hand and gently pet the side of his face. Her fingers crossed over brown-speckled fur, up the slender angle of his jaw. When he took a step forward, her hand moved to the coarse fur of his neck, fingers sliding from brown patch to brown patch with each stroke.

The sound of the barn door opening startled all three, sending Ruke scurrying to the corner of his stall. Evangeline drew back her hand as Caster started for the stairs. "I guess that settles introductions for the day. We'll get back to the goats so the vet can check him over. Hey, Ash," he greeted when they reached the ground level.

Ash, hands full with a bale of alfalfa hay, returned the greeting with a nod before turning her eyes to Evangeline. "Keep your distance from Ruke. He's not yours." Her tone was sharp, eerily reminiscent of Edith Frost's.

Evangeline took in a breath, wondering if it was worth the effort to respond to the unexpected and unwelcomed remark. "I was just looking," she eventually replied.

"Look from a distance. I've been working with him for months and the last thing I need is some temp chick coming in and messing things up."

"Ash, chill out," Caster chimed in, gesturing for Evangeline to join him at the door. "You ain't the boss here. What crawled up your—"

"Bite me, Caster. The same goes for you, too." Ash dismissed them both by turning on her heel and stalking to the back of the barn to start stacking hay bales. Caster only rolled his eyes and headed for the door.

Evangeline followed him out of the barn, glancing back once with regret, wishing she could stay and comfort her new friend during his exam.

THE SLIGHTEST OF BREAKTHROUGHS

JETT KISSED HIS wife on the cheek after helping her finish the dishes, always a time-consuming task after a dinner with the rowdy preserve crew. Usually she pushed him out the door with the rest of them, savoring what little alone time she could find amidst the camp of energetic animals and humans, but tonight they enjoyed that time together.

He found the whole motley crew in their usual Friday night hangout, which was nothing more than a shack of a room nestled between two patches of trees and bordered a small pond. The shack was tucked away from the rest of the preserve and housed a pool table, air hockey table, dartboard, and bar that stocked primarily waters, sodas, and juices. Jett and Lettie didn't allow much drinking on their preserve, and felt fortunate that their keepers and volunteers cherished nights off in one another's company rather than parties and bars off the preserve.

Taking a seat on one of the tattered stools at the makeshift bar, Jett glanced around. Caster was shooting pool with two of the large mammal specialists, Brent and Ash. A group of volunteers that stayed over on the week-ends was already camped out on the couch planning their morning. Tatiana was flipping through a book on native plants, likely coming up with new ideas for enclosures.

"Where's the new gal?" Jett asked the collective over the blaring rock music, not expecting many to answer. In the shack, he wasn't the boss. He was just one of the guys, and that meant being ignored like the rest of them.

"Peaced out after dinner," Caster replied after a few moments' silence. "Haven't seen her since."

"She's probably recovering from a near heart attack," Lana continued. The big cats keeper leaned against the bar and shook her curly-haired head. "I know I still am. I asked her to put out some enrichments in the leopard en-closure since we hadn't let them out yet, and the girl damn near walked into the jaguars, which most certainly *were* out. If Tatiana hadn't of been walking by to stop her, who knows what would have happened. Girlfriend needs to learn her big cats."

This was the first Jett had heard of the incident, and supposed Evangeline didn't say anything for fear of being scolded. "So where is she now?"

"I saw crazycakes by the goats," Ash put in, flipping her long and braided blonde hair over her shoulder before leaning down to line up her shot. "She seems to have a thing for PJ."

Jett bristled at the derision in her voice and insult in her words, but ignored it. For now. Ash was known to have a mouth on her and a hot temper to match, though there was no denying her caring way with the animals, specifically the elephants and giraffes. If not for her extensive knowledge and experience working at a wildlife preserve in Africa, he would have given her the boot long ago for her attitude.

With a sigh, he slid off the stool and left the shack, knowing none of them noticed his sudden departure. As Ash said, he found Evangeline by the goats, illuminated only by white moonlight and pearly stars that reflected off her auburn hair. He stood just outside the enclosure for a moment and watched her. The girl sat cross-legged in the moonlight, her knees pressed up against the chain-link fence, one hand flat against the metal as a goat sniffed at her palm. A look close to serenity was spread across her face, the hint of a smile tugging at the corners of her mouth. For the briefest of moments, Jett felt a tug at his heart and an urge to gather the girl in his arms.

Daughter, his heart told him.

Not yours, his mind argued.

As though sensing his inner argument, Evangeline turned. The tranquil look faded and was instantly replaced by what he'd come to think of as "the wall."

"You're fine," Jett said when she started to rise. He settled down next to her, stretching his long legs out in front of him and leaning back on his palms. "Getting in some quality time with PJ? He's quite the grump."

"I like him," Evangeline answered quietly, stroking the goat's fur through the fence.

Jett peered through the fence at PJ, who was pressed

up against the metal with his head held high, clearly enjoying the attention. It was rare to see the animal so content. "He seems to like you too."

Silence lapsed, a peaceful quiet amidst the sounds of animal calls. Surprisingly, it wasn't uncomfortable, like her silences with other adults had been. They understood one another, even having known each other for only a little over a week. Perhaps more importantly, they understood the need to simply sit without words. For the girl, that meant having time to let her thoughts settle and be at peace with herself. For the man, it meant a break from the daily grind, an escape from having to be the boss for once.

But silences only lasted so long, when so many words needed to be said.

"So," Jett cleared his throat after a while, "why ya sitting out here in the dark? Why not join the gang in the shack? Party's hoppin' there on the weekend nights."

Evangeline kept her eyes on PJ as she pet his black fur. "I'm not part of the gang."

"You're part of the preserve. That makes you part of the gang." Jett chuckled when PJ bleated and pressed his nose against the fence, demanding more attention. "Better watch out. Soon he's gonna call over the rest. Especially Chadster. He's a former show goat and let's just say he still thinks he should be the center of attention." He didn't see any other goats around, though, so he guessed they knew better than to interrupt PJ's attention time. "So ... how have things been so far?"

"Fine."

"Care to elaborate?" When Evangeline cast him a baleful glance, he only lifted a brow. "You're in my care, hon. I have to make sure all is well."

"I said I'm fine."

"I hear ya about had a run-in with one of our fine jaguars." When her back stiffened, Jett only waved a hand at her. "Ah, we'll get ya trained yet on all the different types of animals. So many of them here, they all start to look alike after a while. Caster says you like the goats and giraffes. Maybe we can start focusing you on just those areas, give you more time with them." Jett hid a grin when he saw her eyes widen just a bit. "Course, I need a little bit of leverage, so to speak."

Evangeline huffed, keeping her gaze on PJ. "Like what?"

"Like some proof that doing so will be the best choice for you. So, tell me something about yourself." When the girl didn't answer, Jett tried again. "How about I start?"

He wanted Evangeline to feel comfortable with him, to open up about the traumas of her past in order to work through them, overcome them. Rick had warned him that she was closed off, hiding something, some catalyst to the day she tried to take her life. Jett had made it his mission to discover what was haunting her, and that meant earning her trust by being just as open and honest as he was encouraging her to do.

"Me and Lettie, we have two kids, a boy and a girl," he began, leaning back on his hands and staring up at the night sky. At the preserve, away from the city lights, the stars shone brightly down on them, an entire sky speckled with light and constellations he'd always meant to learn but never actually did. "For years we thought we couldn't have kids. That's what the docs said, anyway, so we stopped trying and instead threw everything we had into this preserve. Then, I don't know. Life threw us a miracle when we least expected it. The boy, Carson, lives a few hours away. Got himself a fancy office job away from shoveling goat droppings. He still comes around often, though. The girl, Lenora, her dream was to be a veterinarian for big game animals. She was a shining star, that one. We lost her to cancer when she was thirteen."

His eyes turned sad at that. Jett looked down at the earth instead of the stars, remembering his daughter in her prime. "It was a hard time, getting over her death. Lettie especially. They were best friends more than they were mother and daughter. They had something special, something I suppose only mothers and daughters can have. If not for this place and all the animals depending on us, I don't know how we would have moved on from Lenora's passing. It made me realize how fragile our lives really are. Any one of us, our time here is just a whisper in the wind. We never know what can happen and we have to take care of the ones who are still here." He suspected Evangeline's mother forgot that last part. "Lenora taught us a lot about love and family. She was a pistol, that one. Always out bossing the keepers around, reminding them of the rules, playing with the animals. She loved the giraffes. You remind me a lot of her, actually. You two are a lot alike."

"I have a father."

The words were snapped out, a warning for the man who may threaten to take the place of another. "I know," Jett replied quietly, running a hand across his beard-roughened chin. "What was he like?"

"He's dead."

"I know," he said again, voice full of affection. "What did you love most about him?"

Evangeline sucked in a breath, not allowing her thoughts to take her back to that day. It was hard to remember her father as he used to be. Images of their last day together — the last moments of his life — always took over memories of happier times.

Stay strong, little elf. Stay strong for me.

"His laugh," she replied in a whisper. "He loved to tell jokes, and then laugh at them, even more than the people he was telling them to. He was always happy." Voices raced through her mind from that day, before the chipper morning turned into something dark and depressing.

"My little elf has a boyfriend."

"Dad!"

"Evie girl and the boy down the street."

"Dad, no way!"

"I heard it all myself. There's no hiding true love from me!"

"Dad, quit it! Come on. Dad. DAD!"

A crash of metal, crunching of doors, the world turned upside down.

Confusion amidst pain. The sky turning to road. Laughter turning into screams.

Skin stained red.

"Evangeline?"

She jumped back to the present, wiping away a tear she hadn't realized had fallen down her cheek. Even now, six months later, she couldn't remember his laugh without the scream.

Evangeline leapt to her feet. "I don't want to talk anymore," she told Jett, who only nodded once at her, before she turned on her heel and all but ran away.

KINDRED SOULS

SHE MET CASTER late the next morning, restless from a night of haunted sleep. She'd made a mistake, opening up to Jett, no matter how small her admission. To admit the truth, any truth about her former life, was to take too many steps backward. To be vulnerable, to let someone see that innermost part of her, was a weakness.

It wouldn't happen again.

"You're late," Caster reprimanded when he saw her approach.

"Sorry," she muttered in response, following him when he started for the giraffe enclosure. "Trouble sleeping."

"They have pills for that."

"I don't need pills."

"Hey, you never know. They might make you more pleasant."

Evangeline glanced up sharply to see Caster grinning over at her, clearly already over her tardiness. She merely shrugged off her annoyance and waited until they were inside the barn to ask her question. "How is Ruke?"

Caster frowned, any pleasure he'd felt at riling her up earlier fading away. They came to a stop in front of Ruke's stall. The giraffe had access to the exterior area, but was preferring the comfort of inside for the day. "Ruke is … Well, he's kind of a special case. There's nothing wrong with him, per say. Nothing medical, at least."

Evangeline cast him a sidelong glance. "What does that mean?"

"It means he's basically in mourning." Caster offered Ruke a handful of lettuce, but the animal merely stared at it from afar. "He had himself a girlfriend for a few years. All the gals here are his, but this one was special. She came from a zoo on the east coast that had been shut down and was here temporarily until we could get her transported to a preserve in Africa. They spent all their time together. It was actually kind of weird, since you don't normally see that kind of behavior with giraffes. He'd get antsy when they weren't together and vice-versa. A few months ago we were able to send her to Kenya, where she's being rehabbed back into the wild at a preserve out there. Ruke stayed since he's part of our breeding program. He's barely been eating, drinking, or sleeping since."

"He misses her."

"That's what we figure, all things considered. Vet can't find anything medically wrong, so we guess he's a bit heartbroken."

Evangeline looked through the bars at Ruke, who was standing in the corner of his stall, a pile of hay at his feet. He wasn't looking at her, but appeared deep in thought in a world all his own. For a moment she wondered what it was giraffes thought about — a tasty snack, memories of home in the wild free, or, perhaps, the ones who held their hearts.

"Hey, snap to it," Caster's voice cut into her pondering. Evangeline looked over to see him holding out a shovel. "You can start over there," he gestured with his head to one of the empty stalls, "and I'll be in the next one over."

SHE SHOVELED COMPOST, hauled hay, and scrubbed stall walls for the better part of three hours. All the while, she remained trapped in her head, thinking too many thoughts, feeling too many emotions. Evangeline was still rattled by her conversation with Jett the night before, no matter how brief. She'd made a mistake confiding in him. Jett wasn't a friend or a shrink or a father figure. He was just her keeper.

Her keeper. The thought made her snort almost in amusement. She really was just another animal in a cage.

It suited her, Evangeline thought. She was where she belonged, trapped in her very own enclosure where she was told what to wear, what to eat, when to work, when to rest. Her time was no longer her own. Life itself no longer belonged to her. Evangeline supposed it was a kind of cosmic justice, karma coming for her after all.

You deserve to be in jail for what you've done.

Her mother's bitter voice rang through her ears, encouraging the girl to shovel another pile of manure, the scrape of metal against concrete drowning out the words in her head. Sweat mixed with dried urine, the stench of human and animal merging into one solitary being.

I am like them, Evangeline pondered, taking a moment's break to glance over at Ruke. The gentle giant was in mourning, grieving for a lost love. They weren't so different after all. Height, color, diet, species itself — such were just details to kindred souls who understood the meaning of heartache and melancholy.

Kindred souls. Evangeline repeated the phrase in her mind, wondering if that was where the name of the Second Hides Program came from. A kindred link between hurting souls, transformations from one mourning body to something else, something light and happy and free. Connecting human to animal, bridging that gap to find some kind of common ground. And in doing so … what? That part she hadn't figured out yet. She may have felt a connection with Ruke, but what did that matter, in the grand scheme of things? Were they able to help one another, or were they just lost in the same pit of despair, separated by a language barrier of the animal kind?

Considering that very fact, Evangeline leaned the shovel against the wall and made the short trek up the metal stairs until she was eye level with Ruke. The giraffe stared at her from his place against the far wall. The two never broke eye contact as she leaned against the railing and watched him curiously for a moment before speaking.

"I bet they tell you not to be sad," Evangeline whispered, frowning at her own words. "I bet they say it's time to move on and make something of yourself. That it wasn't your fault. People go away and we can't get them back and you just have to deal with it. I bet they look at you like you're broken and nothing in the world will ever put you back together again."

She paused for a breath, surprising herself at the small speech. She hadn't spoken that much, for that long, in months. It was refreshing, even if the one listening couldn't understand her.

Or can he? she asked herself when Ruke shifted and slowly approached her, just out of arm's length. His large eyes took in all of her for a moment, then he shook his head. She wasn't sure if it was a dismissal or a language too foreign for her to comprehend.

"I guess they're right, in a way," Evangeline continued, toying with a branch one of the keepers had left on the railing, likely hoping Ruke would eat it while they weren't there. "I guess at some point you have to move on, be normal again. But … how do you go back? What if you can't? I ruined everything. At least yours wasn't your fault." Her voice shook at that and lowered another octave, just as a tear slid down her cheek.

"I—"

Her voice cut off when Ruke leaned over suddenly and wrapped his tongue around the branch, tugging it from her grip. Eyes wide, breath lost, she could only watch him chew slowly on the vegetation as though considering the taste. When he swallowed, Evangeline moved just as slowly, pulling another piece from the bucket at her feet and holding it over the railing, not daring to touch him. Ruke accepted the offering, coming just a little bit closer with each branch, until he was standing mere inches away from his new favorite person.

From his place three stalls over, Caster watched the entire exchange, wonder filling him. He was too far away to hear everything Evangeline whispered to the animal, but the snatches he caught made him question just what was wrong with the troubled teenager who'd found her way to his preserve — what was wrong, and who had caused her trouble.

Something that felt like affection tugged at him when Ruke ate from her hand — an act he rarely allowed anyone else to do. Branch after branch she fed him, and when he'd had enough, the giraffe retreated to his corner, out of the sunlight. Caster turned away when he saw Evangeline about to descend the stairs.

She'd achieved a small miracle, but the moment was meant to be entirely her own.

THE GOAT GODDESS

"I'M TELLING YOU, Jett. She's a damn giraffe whisperer. And a goat one, for that matter. They … listen to her, or something."

Jett chuckled, plucking an apple from the bowl in the center of the kitchen table. "Sounds like you're a bit taken in with the lass."

"Please. She's grumpier than PJ." Caster rose from the table and crossed his arms in a huff. "I'm just saying, it's weird. The giraffes don't listen to us like that. Why her?"

"Uh-huh." Jett waved a hand at Caster, though his words rang through his mind. It was weird, and something to keep an eye on. If Evangeline could help Ruke — something they'd all been trying to do for the past three months and continued to fail at miserably — then the girl truly was a force to be reckoned with. "Get her out with the goats today. We're putting Lady and Ruke out today, see if they take a liking to one another."

"Don't count on it," Caster replied before ducking outside.

He found Evangeline in her usual spot, sitting with her knees against the goat fence and her palm flat against the metal. "You could just go in the pen and pet them, you know."

"I know." She liked it there, outside of the fence, connecting with an animal on the inside, though she couldn't explain why.

"Come on. Those glorious goat droppings won't clean themselves up." He gave her a wry grin and held out a bucket, dropping it back to his side almost immediately. "Sorry. You don't have to carry it."

Indignation filled her, shame threatened to smother. "I'm fine," she snapped, wrenching the bucket out of his hand. The tight grip caused pain to shoot through her fingers but still she held firm, lifted her chin, and all but flounced into the goat pen.

Caster watched her go, not bothering to hide the smirk. He could see the pain written clearly in her eyes. The girl didn't have a poker face to save her life. Still, he admired her chagrin and determination to keep moving, despite the agony she felt, even if her delivery was a bit irritating.

Evangeline felt his eyes on her, which only spurred her forward. She would not let them see how weak she was. She would be strong for herself, for the goats. The animals needed her, even if her mother didn't.

"We'll work here 'til lunch," Caster told her. "Jett wants to keep you here all day, but I figure we can find something else to do after lunch that isn't shoveling out gravel."

"I do what Jett says."

"I don't."

She straightened from the bucket she'd been filling with hay. Curiosity had her asking, "Why not?"

Caster shrugged. "Cuz I can get away with it." At her confused stare, he laughed. "He's my uncle. He didn't tell you?"

"No."

"Well, he's probably just jealous that he can't compare to how clearly awesome I am."

When Evangeline ignored him, Caster was nearly embarrassed by his mocking declaration. He decided not to be annoyed by the girl's lacking sense of humor and instead simply shrugged away the sensation and returned to his work.

The morning passed with just the sounds of boots crunching over crushed rock between them. Sunlight beamed down on them, reminding the duo of the season's unrelenting heat, mocking them with the promise of a summer they wouldn't get to enjoy. Goats milled around them, bleating when they wanted attention and head-butting one another over the hay buckets. Evangeline kept an eye on them, making sure they didn't get too rough, and keeping their food and water clean whenever they made a mess of them. The water bowls, which were installed in all the enclosures, in particular kept her busy, as she was slightly fascinated by them and that interest made her linger on her tasks. She hadn't yet figured out how they worked, but they refilled constantly on their own, some sort of sensor triggered when the water level was too low. Refilling themselves didn't keep the hay and dirt out, though.

Twice Caster considered asking Evangeline if she needed help, but one glance in her direction told him she was determined to do her work on her own, no matter the consequences. Her refusal to accept help grated on his nerves, but for his own sanity's sake he kept to himself. She'd learn soon enough that everyone on the preserve had to ask for help at one point or another. It was the way the place worked, how it ran so well, by having everyone working together. He could excuse her for now, knowing she'd learn that lesson sooner or later, but when she stepped up on a rock to brush off rogue strands of hay, he decided to speak.

"That's PJ's rock," he told her.

Evangeline paused, standing on top of the rock in its center, holding a handful of hay. "So?"

"So, it's PJ's rock," Caster repeated, gesturing with a hand to the goat whose interest had suddenly been caught. "He doesn't like it when people are on it. Or goats, for that matter."

She glanced around, noting that PJ certainly was giving her a strange look. The rock was only a few inches off the ground, but had clearly been claimed. PJ bleated at her and the sound was filled with such annoyance that she smiled.

Caster saw the smile but didn't comment on it. The moment was rare, not to be adulterated with declarations of praise. In some ways he had to consider her behavior like he did the animals' — easily spooked, wary, in need of nurturing but on its own terms. "I'm telling ya, you're gonna get it."

"He won't hurt me."

"He will. He's a grumpy little ass."

"He won't hurt me," Evangeline repeated, sure of herself and wanting to prove it to the annoying man always telling her what to do. "I'm the goat goddess."

A few seconds of silence passed. "You're what?" Caster asked, not sure he heard her correctly. The admission was so weird and random that he had to have heard wrong.

"I'm the goat goddess."

Caster laughed, not able to help himself. "Well, you're certainly something." And she was. Standing on the rock, hands on her hips, something close to a grin crossing her youthful face, Evangeline Frost had become a goddess in her own right.

"You better claim your status then, because someone is looking to take it away from you."

Evangeline glanced over her shoulder at PJ, who had taken a few steps closer to the rock. He wasn't looking at her anymore, but she could tell she was being watched out of the corner of his eye. Something was brewing in that furry head of his, and they all knew it.

"Tell that goat who you are."

"I am the goat goddess."

Caster lifted a brow at her soft response, which was slowly turning hesitant. "That's the best you got? Pretty sure only the delicate little flowers heard you."

Evangeline held her arms out to the sides and tilted her head back. "I am the goat goddess!" Her voice rang out loud and clear, filling the late-morning air, matched only by Caster's supportive cheer.

The moment of triumph ended, though, when PJ met her declaration with a bleat all his own and rammed his head into her knee.

Her bad knee buckled and Evangeline crumpled, the rock striking her in so many different places that she just felt pain. And yet, that pain was mingled with a laugh that threatened to spill out over the quick and quiet groan as she lifted herself to her knees.

Strong arms wrapped around her, helping her off the rock. For a moment she was forced to lean against him until she could put pressure on her knee again, or enough to limp out of the enclosure. Caster led her into the small building off the pen that housed the goat food and other supplies that either sat on shelves or hung on pegs drilled into the walls. He closed the door so the goats couldn't get in. "Damn, girl. When I said stake your territory I didn't mean get into a goat fight."

Evangeline sat on the counter next to the sink, letting him inspect her wounds. "Sorry."

"No need to be sorry. It was kind of funny to watch." He laughed, and chuckled again when he saw the indignation in her eyes. "Come on, you just got knee-checked by a pygmy goat."

She couldn't help it; the laugh threatening to bubble up finally did spill over. It was a short chuckle, barely an amused breath of air, but it was the first she'd felt in six months, let alone actually allowed to escape.

"Hey, what do you know, the new girl can laugh after all."

And in an instant, the light-heartedness faded and reservation took its place.

He saw the unfortunate transformation but knew better than to comment on it. Instead, Caster inwardly cursed himself while reaching for the first aid kit. "No, stay," he commanded when she made a move to jump off the counter. "I need to clean those wounds. If you're good I might even give you a treat."

Evangeline glanced in the mirror over his shoulder to see that he was right. During the fall she'd somehow managed to scrape her elbow, and a shallow cut traced her temple. She didn't remember hitting her head.

Caster cleaned her up quickly and quietly, not allowing his eyes to linger on the scar that traced along her jaw. He wanted to ask about it even though he already knew, or could guess, where it came from. After wiping away the blood and sticking on a few bandages, he moved away so she could hop down. "Alright, goat goddess, you're good to go. Keep off the rocks."

She hopped down and muttered, "Thanks," before scurrying out the door.

He wasn't sure whether she was embarrassed or angry. Either way, Caster knew she'd had some sort of breakthrough, and they had PJ to thank for it.

GROUND HAD BEEN gained, a step taken toward a future filled with promise. Caster took advantage of that progress, not allowing her the time to reflect on the moment and retreat back inside herself.

"Come on," he said, holding out a hand and knowing she wouldn't take it. "I want to show you something in the woods." At her dubious frown, he laughed. "Get your mind out of the gutter. This is fun, I promise. Unless you'd rather get back to shoveling goat shit."

Evangeline looked over her shoulder back at the goat pen. PJ was standing on his rock, eyes locked on her. She almost grinned before she remembered the throbbing in her knee. Glancing back at Caster, she saw that he was already walking away, likely assuming that she would follow.

He was right. She wasn't interested in shoveling and was a little intrigued by what he wanted to show her. Even though this unknown something was *in the woods*, as he'd said, she figured she could trust him. So, she followed silently as they walked along the outskirts of the preserve, past a few of the larger game enclosures, around the back of the shack, and to the edge of the woods. Caster kept on walking into the trees, curving around what looked to Evangeline like a fallen tree covered in years' worth of bramble. She wanted to ask what he was doing, but instead kept in his footsteps, which led behind the fallen tree to a narrow but well-used path.

Evangeline stopped at the foot of the path, not trusting where it would lead. All she saw up ahead were more woods, spotted with sunlight and shadows. "What is this?"

Caster turned around. "A path. Come on. I'm not leading you to your doom. We like to hang out at this place sometimes, especially on our days off, get away from Jett and Lettie and let loose somewhere outside of the shack. It's our own secret hideaway."

His boyish enthusiasm urged her forward. They

walked in silence, Caster in the lead, for the better part of an hour before the narrow path opened up. Pushing away a thorny branch and making a face at the patch of mud she'd just stepped in, Evangeline peered out at the sight before her through wide hazel eyes. She didn't know what she'd been expecting, but this – this wasn't it.

A clearing carpeted with bright green grass just past the wooded pathway gave way to a small swimming hole, the water so clear she could see the rocks beneath the surface and fish swimming in the crystalized depths. The water itself was a sparkling teal, reflecting a gorgeous mix of baby blue sky and emerald aquatic plants. The hue was one she committed to memory, hoping to one day recreate this scene in a painting. Already her mind was working on the right oils to mix that would result in that fascinating and vibrant color.

Along the edges of the lake were patches of ankle-high wildflowers broken up by large slate-gray rocks. Those same smooth rocks were scattered in the lake, and judging by the reflections she could tell the water was much deeper than it seemed from a distance.

At the far end of the lake rose a fascinating structure somehow built into the earth and made of stone. The formation towered above her, enormous gray boulders piled against one another to form a kind of cliffside in the middle of the woods. Vegetation was spotted throughout cracks between the rocks and water trickled from those crevices, making her wonder how exactly this mysterious lake worked.

Evangeline's brows lifted when she saw Caster heading up the side of the slope, carefully picking his way around the rocks. He'd kicked off his shoes and discarded his shirt at the base of the stone structure, climbing with ease up each new level. It only took him a few minutes to reach the top, and it was then that she realized his intention — he was going to jump the long fall into the water.

"Come on!" he yelled down at her, holding his arms out to his sides. "You chicken?"

She huffed, knowing he was only trying to goad her into joining him so she would either be forced to jump or be teased later for backing out. But Evangeline had grown up in South Florida in a community that celebrated surfing, ATVing, and general tomfoolery. That word, *Chicken*, wasn't one she was willing to introduce to her vocabulary. She'd once been known for being "one of the guys" who was always willing to hit the trails on a dirt bike or start up a game of flag football on the beach. Jumping off a rock into a pool of water below was not something that scared her.

To prove it, she began the climb, first kicking off her shoes for better balance with her bare toes. She made it about halfway before realizing the slope was steeper than she thought, and less forgiving with its smooth rocks and sparse handholds. Six months ago that wouldn't have been a problem, but gripping the hard stone with her bad hand and putting pressure on her already damaged knee was proving difficult. This she refused to admit, and so farther up she climbed, breathing through the pain that started in her palm and webbed out into her fingers.

Wrist.

Forearm.

Body.

A gasp escaped when a spasm had her hand going limp — and her grip with it. For a moment she felt frozen in air, the world around her existing only in heightened senses. The sound of rocks shifting and sliding clacked through her head. The feel of her feet slipping across stone shuddered through her. The sight of cliffside stretching away from her backward-falling body sent terror racing through her thoughts.

She felt the hand on her wrist before she saw the one who caught her — Caster, with a firm grip on her arm, drawing her closer to the edge, and finally up and over.

"You trying to give me a heart attack?" he asked, attempting to hide his fear with a laugh. "What the hell happened?" His harsh tone faded when he saw the way she massaged her hand. "Well, you're okay. No harm done. Just don't tell Jett or Lettie. They'd kill me if they found out I almost killed you."

Trying to push back the shame at almost having fallen, Evangeline walked to the edge of the cliff and peered down at the blue water below. The drop didn't look too far to her, though not knowing just how deep the water was did give her reason to hesitate. "They don't know about this place?" she asked, finding it hard to believe the heads of the preserve knew nothing of a watering hole of sorts in the middle of the woods. *Their* woods.

"Nah, they're so busy with the animals that they don't get out much. We only come out here when we know we won't be missed for a few hours." Caster sat down on a rock close to the edge and patted the spot beside him. "Have a seat and give me your hand."

"Why?"

"Because I want to propose and this is the most romantic spot for it." Caster shook his head with a smirk. "Jesus, will you lighten up? This isn't some teen romance flick. Just sit down and stop being a pain in the ass."

She wanted to be offended, at the very least indignant, but decided she wouldn't give him the pleasure of proving him right. Evangeline sat down next to him, barely stopping herself from rolling her eyes, and held out her right hand. Caster took it wordlessly and began massaging, gently pressing his thumbs in the center of her palm and working his way out to the fingertips. She had to force herself not to cringe at his touch, not to think about the physical therapists who had scolded her as much as they had helped her for not doing the exercises on her own. After a while she suspected they blamed her for her lack of healing, which was part of the reason why she stopped going. *You have to push yourself*, they told her, over and over again. *Things will never be the same*, she responded each time, unable to do what they asked. Looking back on it, she knew she had merely been projecting her own insecurities, but still, at times it was easier to place the blame on someone, anyone, else.

Evangeline watched his hands, amazed by his gentleness and mesmerized by the fact that whatever he was doing, it was working. The pain was receding, slowly at first but receding nonetheless. The fact that the ache was turning into a light throb distracted her enough from the other fact — that she was only an arm's length away from a half-naked guy she refused to admit was attractive. Her eyes scanned over his bare chest and toned shoulders before locking on her hand again. "Where did you learn massage therapy?"

"With Lettie," Caster replied, pretending not to notice the way she not-so-subtlety checked him out. "Her daughter, my cousin, always wanted to be a vet and got it in her head that to be a good vet she had to be good with people too, so she read up on massage therapy to help her mom. Lenora used to help with the arthritis and she showed me how to do it when she got sick. Without telling Lettie, of course. Lenora, she was only thirteen but she was more mature than any kid I've ever met. She knew she wasn't going to make it through the cancer and she wanted to make sure someone was able to take care of Lettie. It couldn't be Jett. He was too broken up about just the idea of losing his daughter. When it actually happened, it about killed him too. Their son kind of kept to himself and left for college not soon after, so it was just Jett and Lettie for a long time, trying to get by."

Evangeline's eyes scanned his face, noting the sadness there. Lettie and Jett had lost a daughter, but Caster lost someone he was also close to, a cousin loved as a sister. "I'm sorry."

"Thanks. It was hard for a while, but we got through it. I think the preserve helped them, working with the animals. And I help Lettie when I can. I figure it's the least I can do for Lenora." He shifted, a bit uncomfortable with the personal talk now that it was focused on him. "So, if you don't mind me asking, what happened here?"

Evangeline sighed, not wanting to answer but knowing she owed him the truth. "It's from the accident." Guessing the answer wasn't good enough based on the brow he raised, she continued, "It's not like it's a secret that I was in a car accident and … what happened as a result. I had a lot of injuries."

"Like what?" he asked softly when she paused. His thumbs moved to her wrist, massaging lightly.

"Broke my knee, got my face all cut up, broke my

hand in a few places." She gestured to the various parts of her body, one finger trailing the scar along her jaw. "I used to be an artist, but I can't hold a brush anymore. People thought I'd do it professionally. So much for that."

Caster considered her words. He'd noticed the slight limp, which seemed to progress as the day went on, likely due to overuse. He'd also wondered about the scar and saw the way she tried to hide it by letting her long hair cover that side of her face. "Didn't you go to physical therapy afterwards?"

"For a little bit."

"Why not until everything was healed?"

"You're fine. It will heal. This is your punishment for the crash. Stop complaining about what you deserve."

Her mother's words rang through her ears, silencing Evangeline. She couldn't answer the question, wouldn't answer it. Wouldn't admit the truth that her mother refused to take her to therapy, to pay for it. Eventually Evangeline had given up and started to believe the words that were said to her every night.

This is your punishment.

Stop complaining.

I wish it had been you, not him.

Trapped by the words that had broken her, Evangeline couldn't find an answer to Caster's question, so instead she said nothing.

Caster sensed he'd touched a nerve. He wanted to ask more but decided to go for the easier question. "So ... you ready to jump, or you gonna be chicken?"

Eager to get away from his questions — and his touch — Evangeline jumped up from the rock. She crossed her arms and attempted a glare, though the corners of her mouth threatened to turn upward. "You first."

"But of course." Not able to resist the chance to further rile her up, Caster added, "Don't forget to lose the shirt."

Her arms tightened across her chest. "Not happening."

He tossed her a boyish grin before taking his place at the edge of the cliff. "See ya at the bottom. You better not chicken out on me." With a cheer he jumped off the cliff, cannon-balling into the water with a splash.

Evangeline leaned over the edge and watched him fall, nervous until she saw him resurface. He waved up at her, taunting her again that she would chicken out.

Not bothering to hide her smile, Evangeline met his taunt and leapt off the cliff into the waiting water below.

A FORGOTTEN CHILD

AN UNEXPECTED BUT welcomed sense of happiness filled Evangeline as she headed back to the big house for dinner, Caster at her side. Both were still a bit damp and needed to change, but the dinner bell had been rung and tardiness was not acceptable. There were a few stares and winks as they entered, the keepers knowing where they had been, Lettie confused by their wet hair.

"Goats made a mess," Caster said before she could ask, as though the answer explained everything. Evangeline was surprised when the older woman accepted the reply with a shrug and turned back to the stove.

Dinner passed in its usual manner, the gang discussing their day and Evangeline retreating back inside her mind. She'd never felt like part of the group, though Caster did his best to keep her in the loop by including her in his recount of the day and encouraging her to share funny stories about the goats, though she noted he left out the part about PJ knocking her off his rock. She silently wondered why, ultimately deciding he didn't want her to be embarrassed by the incident, though she considered that, just maybe, he didn't say anything because it was a moment just the two of them shared, much like their leap off the rock.

Having a moment just for them nearly made her smile, before she remembered that soon, those moments would end and she would be just another teenager who passed through the preserve. And when she was gone, they would be back to just their original group, as though she'd never made an appearance. Her company was temporary, and she had to keep it as such. Part of her supposed she simply didn't want to be part of them, that she didn't deserve to be. She didn't understand most of their talk anyway, with its animal- and preserve-specific lingo and inside jokes she wasn't privy to. It was only natural that she kept her distance.

After dinner, Evangeline waited until the others had left before approaching Jett. She wrung her hands together nervously, biting her bottom lip while formulating the question in her mind.

"Um, Jett?" she asked, interrupting the man as he helped Lettie with the dishes.

"How can I be of assistance?" he asked with a grin, turning and wiping his hands on a towel. "I hope it's something you need help lifting or moving so I can get out of dish duty."

"Don't count on it," Lettie said over her shoulder.

Evangeline attempted a smile, but shook her head. "No, um … I was wondering if I could use the phone to call my mom. I don't have a cell phone."

"That all? You don't even have to ask! Phone's in the front hallway." Jett gestured toward the front of the house. "Take as long as you need."

"Thanks." She nodded and scurried away to the small alcove in the foyer, picking up the phone before she could change her mind.

Hesitation had her hand hovering over the numbers, fingers poised to dial but nerves keeping them still. Voices of the past haunted her present, reminding her why she was there, why her mother was so happy to see her go. A word crossed her mind – *unwanted* – a revelation of her life's worth.

Annoyance and spite had her fingers dialing the number she knew best; fear had her holding her breath as the *ring, ring, ring* of the telephone vibrated in her ear. Just when she thought her efforts had been in vain, the line picked up.

"Hello?"

Evangeline nearly hung up before she replied, "Hi, Mom."

The woman on the other end was silent for a moment. "What do you need?"

"Nothing. I mean, nothing bad or anything." Evangeline bit back a sigh, trying to keep the conversation pleasant. "I just wanted to talk, see how you were doing."

"I'm fine."

She waited for more, and got none. "How is work?"

"Fine."

"Have you gone out at all? Had fun?"

"I said I'm fine."

Evangeline leaned against the wall, hunched over as though attempting to protect herself from outside stares that didn't even exist. "Well … It's nice here, I guess. There are a lot of animals. They are letting me work with the giraffes, which—"

"Did you need something?" Edith cut in, causing Evangeline to pause and suck in a deep breath, one filled with hesitation and the threat of tears.

"Um, not really, I guess. I just wanted to say hi and that I miss you." Hope burned in her chest, a silent prayer that the sentiment would be reflected in the elder version of her own self. The flame fizzled when she heard the sigh on the other end.

"I have to go."

"Okay." Evangeline chewed on her bottom lip. "I hope I can see you soon. Maybe you can come to visit?"

"I don't have time for whatever it is you want. I have to go."

For long after the line went dead, Evangeline held the phone to her ear. Her mind replayed the brief conversation over and over again, hoping to hear something different each time. Finally the phone fell from her hand, forgotten on the floor as she walked outside in a zombie-like trance. She knew not where she was going, only that she had to escape the suffocating emptiness of a house filled with strangers.

The night welcomed her with its shadows and sounds, cloaking her, hiding her from the truth of what her family had become. The clouded black sky above mocked her with its expansive darkness, whispering all the doubts she had about herself into her mind.

Alone.

Broken.

Unwanted.

Into the preserve she wandered, no destination in mind and yet pulled forward by a hand she couldn't identify — a guiding hand that brought her to the giraffe enclosure. The main barn door was locked, so she tried the window. Grim satisfaction filled her when she discovered it was unlocked. It took her less than a minute to crawl inside and find her way to Ruke's stall. A single overhead light was on in the corner of the barn, giving off enough of an orange glow to let her see the way.

The giraffe was awake, though not pleased by the interruption. He eyed Evangeline suspiciously as she stalked up the stairs to his stall and propped herself up on the ledge. Deciding she was too restless to sit, she jumped down and began to pace, first across the small ledge at the top of the stairs and then back down the steps in the space in front of Ruke's stall. All the while she felt the giraffe's eyes on her, assessing and comforting her in a way only animals could.

"I just wanted to see if she remembered," Evangeline whispered, telling herself that in some strange way Ruke could understand her. She needed that, needed *someone* to understand, even if they couldn't talk back. "I just wanted to see if she would talk to me."

But she didn't. Edith Frost wanted nothing to do with her daughter, not able to spare more than two minutes on a phone call with the only child she had, the child she hadn't seen in nearly a month.

"She hates me. She wishes … she wishes for Daddy and not me. It's all my fault." The misery that had been building since her mother hung up on her started to twist, turn, morph into something dark and dangerous. "She wishes *this* had worked."

Evangeline held up her left arm, ripping off the bracelet and showing Ruke the scar that stretched vertically from her wrist three inches up. It was an ugly scar, ugly and bruised and welted to match her heart. The doctors said it would fade in time, but time was too fresh right now, when the wounds on her soul couldn't compete with healing that would only come in the future.

"I just want it to be over," Evangeline vented, pressure building in her chest, unexplained energy pleading for an outlet. "I want Mom to like me again and hang out with me. I want to be remembered like I used to be, not for what I did. I don't want it to be my fault anymore. I want everyone to know the *truth* but they can't because I can't do that to *him*!"

She accented the last word with a punch to the barn wall, sending her right fist into the wood. Only once before had she ever felt so angry, so defeated, that she responded with violence and vented her fury on an unsuspecting wall. But unlike that other instance, this time she couldn't stop. And unlike that other wall, this one wasn't as forgiving.

Again and again she punished the wall for the emotions she couldn't suppress, overcome, kill. Again and again she forced away her thoughts and focused only on that single spot on the wood, the spot dented with the force of her fist, the spot now coated in a thin layer of her own blood.

A red haze coated her vision, blinding her from her actions, not allowing her to feel the pain in her hand when it struck wood or sliced through glass. The roaring in her ears didn't let her hear the clatter of a table overturned or the shouts of panic outside as a door was rattled open. Only the rage reigned, no longer locked away and hidden, finally allowed a moment to unleash itself on the world.

This was punishment, punishment for the entire world that had shut her out, refused to forgive, blamed the child who only wanted her father to live so she could take his place. This was acceptance, acceptance for the pain she deserved, finally giving in to the emptiness and forgetting who she was so she could, for once, not have to feel anything at all.

It wasn't until a pair of arms wrapped around her shoulders and yanked her away from the wall that Evangeline realized she was still moving, that tears were streaming down her cheeks, that her throat ached from a scream she didn't remember releasing. Instinctively her body fought against the arms, struggling to break free of a hold too strong for her broken body. Only her mind could fight, try to make sense of the cage around her. The feel of a rough beard against her shoulder told her it was Jett who had come for her, Jett who was soothing her in that deep voice of his, Jett who had sunk with her to the barn floor and was rocking her back and forth like a child as she wept.

And she let him.

JETT SANK INTO a chair at the kitchen table, gratefully accepting the mug of tea Lettie pressed into his hands.

"Tell me from the beginning," she insisted, taking a seat across from him.

"I'm not entirely sure where that is," he replied tiredly. It had taken a couple hours to calm the girl down enough to move from the barn, and another hour before she was settled in her bed, lying on her side and staring blankly at the wall like she'd just been given a lobotomy. "She asked if she could use the phone to call her mother, and I said yes. You saw that part. Then I started walking my rounds for the night after we finished up cleaning the kitchen. Didn't think anything of her calling, to be honest. What harm could it do? Anyway, next thing I know Ash is calling on the walkie telling me she heard a noise in the barn and thought it was Evangeline. Well, you know Ash. Called her something not quite as nice as her name, but anyway. Said it sounded like she was tearing the place apart. So I came running and sure enough, she was in there wailing away on the wall like it was her own worst enemy."

He replayed the moment in his mind, glancing through the open barn window to see the girl in a blind panic as she let loose one punch after the next. As if driven by a demon sitting on her shoulders, he recalled thinking. That vision scared him, not for the damage she'd caused to the barn, or to herself, but for whatever it was that had brought her to that point.

"So, I get in there and pull her away. She's got a bloody hand, crying, screaming about something but I couldn't make out what. Truth be told, I don't think she even knew she was talking or crying. She just cried, harder than I've ever seen anyone cry, Lettie. She fought me at first then seemed to realize I wasn't gonna hurt her. Just sat there in my arms and let the floodgates open. I finally got her off the floor and into her room, but it's like she didn't even know where she was. I wanted to say something, but … Hell, I don't know what to say to the girl. I don't even know what happened."

Lettie took in a deep breath, pondering the situation. Evangeline was a quiet girl, but not the kind of quiet one had to watch out for. Of that much, she was certain. The teenager's hesitance was born out of habit, not anything malicious. "Well, clearly something with her mother triggered it. The question is, what?"

Jett nodded and took a sip of tea. "That certainly is the question."

AN ENEMY IS MADE

"IT'S OKAY, EVANGELINE. It's okay. Calm down."

"Let it out. Let it go."

"Take a breath, Evie girl."

"Easy, now. You're safe here. I've got you."

She awoke to Jett's voice in her ears, memories of the night before both shaming and alarming her. Evangeline rolled over onto her back, blinking sleep from her eyes, struggling to clear the fog that had settled over her mind so she could understand the truth of what she'd done. For a while she simply stared up at the faded wooden ceiling, counting the lines in the beams to distract herself from the memories of last night, of the barn, of herself.

But there was no escaping her actions.

She'd let her mother influence her, let that same hate

and fear and hopelessness she'd fought so hard to ignore take over her body. The result of that was, at the least, property damage that she would find a way to fix; at the most, it was several steps backward to the ones she'd thought she had taken forward. And for what? One short phone call, one even shorter conversation.

She wanted her mother to talk to her, to be there for her. But that single, short conversation told her what she needed to know — that she was alone. Irrevocably, unforgettably, alone.

"Easy, now. You're safe here. I've got you."

But Jett had been there, she reminded herself as she observed her hand, frowning at the scabbed and bruised knuckles, wincing at the aching that wound its way through the bones. Jett had pulled her away from the wall, held her arms at her sides even when she fought against him, soothed her until her tears subsided, then tucked her into bed with a gentle kiss to her forehead. Just like her father would have done.

Was that why she let him hold her, speak to her in that soothing voice? Was that why she wasn't as humiliated as she should have been? Did she *want* to let him take on that fatherly role, even if just for one night? Jett had known what to say and when to say it, when to be silent, like he knew her better than she knew herself. He didn't ask her to talk about it — yet. She would have to answer for last night, but wasn't quite ready to face anyone just yet.

A knock at the door had her groaning internally, fearing the time of reckoning was already upon her. Relief flooded her when she opened the door to see Ash instead of Jett on the other side.

"Breakfast is ready," the keeper, clearly disgruntled judging by the tight frown and rigid stance, informed Evangeline in a curt tone, her brown eyes dark and narrow. "Afterwards you can clean up the mess you made in the giraffe barn. Next time you have a temper tantrum, break your own stuff and leave ours alone. We don't have time for psychotic episodes here. Got it?"

The relief curdled into shame, hot and painful in her gut. Evangeline could only nod, closing the door quietly after Ash gave her one last look of disgust before turning away. Instead of going to the big house for breakfast, Evangeline went back to bed, lying down to stare at the ceiling.

NO ONE CAME for her, which she found odd. The call for breakfast came and went, and still no one but Ash visited for a lecture or conversation. After a few hours Evangeline convinced herself to get out of bed and dress in work clothes, then headed to the barn. She kept to the outskirts of the trails, hoping no one would see or talk to her. Luck was on her side, and she arrived in peace.

The barn was empty when she entered, save for Ruke, who still refused to spend any of his time outside. Evangeline approached the spot from last night, seeing the slight dent in the wood, the dried blood on the wall and splattered on the floor. She was also surprised to see the hay, tools, and supplies spread across the floor. Although she didn't remember slinging any of them off their respective shelves, she knew the mess must have been made by her hands and was completely embarrassed by that fact.

With a resigned sigh, she began cleaning, picking up the loose objects and setting them back in their proper places. She'd been in the barn enough times to know where everything went, or at least offer a best guess. Then she swept up the hay into a large pile, not sure what to do with it, if it would be trashed or reused. The fact that she would have to ask where it went instead of simply moving it embarrassed her further, but it was a just punishment.

When she moved to the wall to scrub away the blood, she heard the barn door open behind her.

"About time," Ash said from the doorway. Evangeline glanced over her shoulder to see the woman standing with her arms crossed, a look of annoyance spread across her face. She guessed Ash was only in her early or mid-twenties, but the look of bitterness permanently spread across her face made her seem much older, and not at all in a flattering way. "No way was I cleaning up this mess."

"I'm sorry," Evangeline replied honestly. "I was ... it won't happen again."

"No, it won't." Ash agreed, leaning against the doorframe. "Because you're out of here." She lifted a single, perfectly manicured brow when Evangeline paused in her scrubbing before resuming her work, never looking back. "Yeah, you heard me. We don't need your kind here. You can go ruin someone else's business. Or better yet, get locked up the next time you act like a goddamn psycho."

A retort burned on the tip of her tongue, but Evangeline bit it back. She wouldn't make this worse. She didn't want to leave, and saying something snotty back to Ash would surely seal her fate more so than it already was. So she kept scrubbing, hoping Ash would go away.

"You don't even need to be in here as much as you are," Ash continued, seeing the tension building in the teenager's arms and shoulders with each word. "The giraffes don't need you talking to them. Talking isn't going to save them. *We* are. *We* know what we're doing, not you and whatever you think you learned when you went to the zoo as a kid. So let us do our job and stay out of our way. You aren't wanted here anyway."

"Ash."

Both Evangeline and Ash turned at the interruption of a third voice. Caster stood just outside the barn, a dangerous expression on his face.

"Can I talk to you?" he asked Ash pointedly. She obliged, closing the barn door behind her after stepping outside. "What the hell is wrong with you?"

"Excuse me?" she laughed. "You can't seriously be defending that nutcase."

"She's not a nutcase. She's been through a rough time."

Ash nodded, eyes narrowed in understanding. "Oh, I see. You've got a little thing for the crazy girl."

"She's sixteen, Ash. I don't have a *thing* for her. But I'm not going to let you treat her that way either." He'd heard everything, or almost everything. "You are twenty-six years old, for Christ's sake. You're acting like you're in high school. It's embarrassing."

Ash glared at him for a moment, her pretty face turning into a mask of resentment. Caster braced himself for a response, knowing of Ash's attitude, and was relieved when she simply turned on her heel and stalked away.

Blowing out a breath, he waited until she disappeared from sight then entered the barn. Evangeline was still scrubbing the wall, with more force than necessary. "She's gone," he told the girl, seeing the way her shoulders relaxed. "And she's wrong, you know. We don't all feel the way she does."

"You should," Evangeline muttered, not caring if he heard.

Caster stepped up to her side. "Why did you take her crap? You could have told her to shut up and get away from you."

"Yeah, right," Evangeline scoffed. She rinsed out the rag in a bucket at her feet, pleased to see that the wall was clean. "Besides, she was right. I deserved it."

"Why would you say that? Hey." Caster caught her by the arm when she tried to walk away from him. "What's going on? You don't really believe that, do you?"

"So what if I do?" she snapped, yanking her arm from his grasp. "I cleaned up the mess. It won't happen again."

She left him standing there, staring after the girl who thought she deserved the worst the world had to offer.

18

A STORM IS BREWING

"CASTER, I'VE TOLD you and Jett before, you need to get Ruke outside."

"And I've told you, he won't go."

Caster and Dr. Bane, the preserve's big game veterinarian, stared at one another, both equally frustrated. They stood in the barn at the railing overlooking Ruke's stall. The vet had spent the better part of two hours with the giraffe, taking his vitals, observing him, writing down notes. The entire time, Caster watched with bated breath, ordering himself not to show any nerves. He knew these visits were necessary, legally required even, but it didn't help when Ruke refused to cooperate.

Dr. Bane gathered his things and walked down the steps. Together the two walked outside and observed the females meandering about in the sunny enclosure. "As I told Jett last time, this type of behavior isn't normal. Ruke has lost a lot of weight that he can't afford to lose, even more since my last visit, and not being in the sun is going to eventually take its toll."

Caster sighed and ran a hand through his dark hair. "We know all this, and we've tried everything. Short of throwing a rope around his neck and dragging him out, I don't know what you expect us to do."

"I expect you to find another solution," the vet answered, pulling out a pen from his white jacket pocket. He wrote down a few notes and handed the piece of paper to Caster. "I want you to start implementing a change in his diet, something with higher protein. Give him a change in his daily routine too. Something to stimulate his mind. Something different that he hasn't seen before that may actually spark his interest. If you can get him outside, then keep him there all day and try to get him moving around, interacting with the other giraffes. He's the only male here, so there's no reason why you can't let him have free reign of the place while the females are out. Who knows, he may even take a liking to one of them like he did his old girl."

Caster kept his expression neutral, though internally he was frowning. *Like we haven't tried all this before*, he thought, not bothering to explain that what Ruke really needed was the giraffe equivalent to depression medication. Or, at the very least, more time. No one quite understood why the giraffe was so melancholy over the loss of a female, considering he'd never been upset over losing one before, but to Dr. Bane depression wasn't the problem. Diet and exercise were clearly to blame.

"I'll be back soon," he told Caster, who only nodded.

"Give Jett and Lettie my best."

CASTER ENTERED THE big house on a mission to find Jett and share his plan. This time of the afternoon, his uncle was typically holed up in his office fielding phone calls from zoos interested in one of their animals or dealing with other business things Caster knew nothing about. Honestly, he had no interest in learning that business side of things. He was perfectly content working with the animals and, perhaps, one day taking on their prospective partnership with African preserves.

He heard voices traveling down the hall, the harsh and hushed tones making him pause. Curiosity had him tiptoeing forward until he was only a few feet away from the office. It wasn't often that there were arguments loud enough for the entire house to overhear, as his uncle was one of the most agreeable people Caster had ever met — sometimes annoyingly so.

"Enough with the attitude," he heard Jett say in what he'd long since thought of as the 'fatherly voice.' "You said what you said, and now you face the consequences."

"What a load of crap, Jett." Caster identified the voice as belonging to Ash and knew instantly what the woman was being confronted about. He'd informed Jett of the encounter himself. "You want to stick your neck out for that freak, then by all means, go for it. But that doesn't mean I have to like the fact that she's here, interrupting *my* day and messing with *my* animals. You never should have let her come here."

"They don't belong to you, Ash. And you are not in control. *I* am. Who I bring on the preserve is not your choice, but you will respect each and every person working here, whether they are being paid or part of the program."

"Oh, right, the *program*," Ash sneered back. Caster could imagine her rolling her eyes as she paced the room. He cringed, already having guessed what she was about to say and adding a preemptive, *Oh, no, she didn't* in his mind. "The precious Second Hides Program. Your pet projects for losers. Getting off to a great start, isn't it?"

"It was working quite well, until you started behaving like a raving lunatic."

Ash scoffed. "I'm the lunatic? Check the medical records, Jett. *I* didn't try to kill myself."

"No," Jett agreed, his tone sad, "but I suspect her attempt was the result of treatment very close, if not identical, to what you so kindly displayed in the barn."

Silence stretched. Caster, thoroughly insulted by the woman's words, almost turned away when Jett spoke again.

"This isn't the first time someone has complained about you, Ash. Your attitude isn't welcome by the others here, and I, for one, am tired of having to put out the fires you start with careless words. So, here's the deal. If you can't treat Evangeline, or anyone else here, with the respect they deserve, then I have no place for you. The choice is yours, Ash."

"How about this for a choice?" Ash spat back. "I—"

"If you say the words, there is no taking them back,"

Jett interrupted with warning.

"Quit," she finished.

Caster ducked around the corner in time for Ash to stalk out of the office, slamming the front door behind her. He counted to thirty in his head before daring to face Jett. When he entered the office he expected to see his uncle sitting at the desk with his head in his hands, as he often did when frustrated, but instead Jett was standing at the window, watching Ash drive away.

"She already had her bags packed," Jett said, knowing his nephew heard the entire exchange. He scrubbed his rough hands over his face wearily. "She came in here ready to quit."

"But why?" Caster took a seat at the desk. "She's been here for six years and she quits because some girl who's been here a month punched the barn wall? It doesn't make any sense."

"It escalated rather quickly," Jett agreed, and Caster had the feeling he was hiding something, another facet of the conversation that hadn't been heard. "We've been butting heads over her attitude for months now. The thing with Evangeline was just the last straw. It will be tough until we can replace her, but this preserve can't afford to have someone so negative on the staff. That girl was turning into a plague of bad moods and bitterness. We'll manage better without her." He returned to his desk and sat down with a sigh. "What did the vet say?"

Though he wanted to ask more about the meeting with Ash, Caster switched gears and recapped the conversation. "He didn't tell us anything we don't already know. I guess now the trick is figuring out how on earth we're supposed to get Ruke to go outside."

"And eat," Jett commented, one finger stroking his beard. He frowned when Caster leaned forward as though suddenly remembering something. "What?"

"About that." Caster leaned back again. "The new girl got him to eat. I'm serious," he said when Jett stared at him skeptically. "She was talking to him about some personal things, just to get it all out, I think. I wasn't supposed to hear what she said, I'm sure, so I stayed out of the way and just watched."

"Well you are a talented eavesdropper," Jett commented wryly.

"One of my many talents." Caster brushed him off with a shrug. "Anyway, she was talking to him all calm and gentle. Then she just started feeding him and he was all over it. They've got something, Jett. Some kind of connection. You want Ruke to go outside and eat, let Evangeline work with him. And I mean really work with him, not just clean out stalls and restock hay feeders."

Jett thought about it, indecision tearing at him. "I don't know, Caster. We need someone with actual animal knowledge in there. Evangeline doesn't know what she's doing. Not to mention she's a bit of a loose cannon."

"Not with him."

Jett lifted a brow at his nephew's insistence. "You want to vouch for her, guarantee we don't have to worry about another barn meltdown?" Caster nodded after only the slightest display of hesitation. "Then go for it. With Ash gone, we need more hands helping with the big game anyway. But you're responsible for her. If this goes south, it's on you."

Caster stood, a grin forming. He wasn't worried at all. "Great. We'll start in the morning. Oh." He stopped on his way out the door. "Speaking of the meltdown, any idea what caused it?"

"An idea," Jett answered, glancing at the file on his desk. "Not sure if I'm right, though."

He hoped he was. After all, he was planning an entire celebration around pure speculation. But if he was right, he had a feeling the entire course of Evangeline's life would change.

HELP THE HELPLESS

CASTER AND EVANGELINE walked almost side by side toward the giraffe barn the next morning, one barely able to contain her excitement and the other enjoying the way his companion for the day tried so hard to remain calm. Evangeline didn't know what was in store for her, but supposed it didn't matter. They were letting her stay *and* allowing her back with the giraffes. Surely she had done something right in her brief time at the preserve. At her side, Caster was pleased by how eager the girl was to work, how happy just the idea of being around the giraffes made her.

"Derek," Caster greeted as they came upon the oldest of the primate keepers. Derek was one of the longest standing employees, having worked at the preserve since its inception after a brief career in the zoo field. He stood at just over six feet with broad shoulders, a weather-worn face, and unruly red hair that was currently being knotted into small spirals by the squirrel monkey on his shoulder.

"Caster," Derek greeted back in a lilted voice. "Who's the fresh face?"

"Oh, right, you were out of town. He just got back from Ireland," Caster explained to Evangeline, who only nodded, though she had been curious about the man's accent. "Derek, this is Evangeline. She's joining us for a bit. Evangeline, this is Derek."

"And Bilbo," Derek put in with a toothy grin, gesturing with his head to the monkey. "Can't forget about Bilbo."

Evangeline offered a half-smile at the name. "Like Bilbo Baggins?"

"The one and only. He's a butthead though," Derek said. "Likes 'ta steal things.'"

"He's still got my belt buckle," Caster replied with a smirk. "I'd like it back, you know."

"Hey, tell him, he's the thief."

Evangeline froze when Bilbo leapt from Derek's shoulder to her own, grasping on to her hair with tiny fingers. She'd never had a squirrel monkey on her before and the feeling was … adorably strange, she decided. She felt tiny feet on her shoulder and even tinier fingers against her scalp. A giggle escaped when Bilbo curled up on her shoulder and rubbed his head against her neck.

"Hey now, little rascal. Don't go getting' all friendly with a lass ya never even met." Derek clapped once and Bilbo jumped to alert, leaping from Evangeline's shoulder and back to Derek. "Sorry about that. He likes hair, and ya got a lot of it."

"It's okay." Evangeline smoothed down the hair Bilbo had mussed. "He's cute."

Derek spared the monkey a glance when Bilbo started chattering loudly. "Yeah, yeah, I heard her. Everyone loves ya." He nodded at the duo again. "Well, back 'ta work. Jett's got a nice long list for me."

"Later," Caster replied with a laugh, then looked over at Evangeline. "So even Bilbo loves you. You got a weird animal sense."

Evangeline shrugged. "You're just jealous."

He only laughed again and continued leading her to the giraffes. When they got to the barn, he brought her inside and started giving her the instructions for the day.

"Okay." Caster rubbed his hands together in anticipation. "The goal is to get Ruke's butt outside and interacting with the others. We've tried everything the past month or so, short of actually forcing him, which Jett and Lettie refuse to do because it may cause him further harm. So far we've just been opening up the skylight over his stall during the day, but the dude needs to get out and run around. Or, you know, just stand there, like they usually do."

Evangeline eyed Ruke, who was staring back at her. "So what do you want me to do?" She was just one person, and not a strong one at that. There would be no giraffe manhandling from her.

Caster blew out a breath. "Well … I'm going to have you do something completely against the rules so don't ever tell anyone about it. And if you ever do tell anyone, I'm gonna deny, deny, deny." At her dubious look, he grinned. "Come on, it'll be fun."

He jogged over to the far wall and pressed a button.

Evangeline watched as a door slid open in Ruke's stall, giving him access to the enclosure outside. Sunlight streamed in through the opening, but the giraffe didn't move.

"What now?"

Caster gestured to Evangeline. "Time to break some rules."

He led her away from the stall and over to another door, one she'd never seen unlocked. The door opened with a creak after he lifted the lever that held it shut. "After you."

Evangeline hesitated, her brow furrowing. "Out into the giraffe enclosure?"

"Sure thing. You're gonna get Ruke outside."

"How?"

"With your special brain powers." When her brow furrowed, Caster only shrugged. "I don't know. That's for you to figure out. All I know is, Ruke likes you and listens to you in a way he doesn't listen to anyone else. So, maybe you can help him."

The thought of helping, possibly saving, the animal got her feet moving. Evangeline stepped through the door, blinking in the bright sunlight. She'd never seen the enclosure from this angle before, slightly lower than the outside perimeter and not looking through a metal fence. Taking a step forward, she imagined herself as a giraffe — albeit an incredibly short one — picturing what she would love most about being out here. The trees were tall and green and full. The grass was a gorgeous verdant carpet. Rock formations scattered throughout mimicked the African terrain. There was shade and sun, lots of food and water, friends to hang out with.

What was missing?

She didn't have that piece of the puzzle, but she knew how to find it. The other giraffes out for the day, four total, watched her as she slowly made her way to Ruke's stall. Evangeline watched them as well out of the corner of her eye, heart beating wildly at the thought of being so close to wild animals. They were called gentle giants, but she knew what one kick from a startled giraffe could do to her ribcage. Or worse, her head.

"Hey, buddy," she said quietly when she came to a stop in front of the stall. Ruke hadn't moved. "You coming out or what?" Glancing over her shoulder, she saw Caster leaning against the barn wall with his arms crossed, taking in the scene.

Evangeline held out her hand, which was grasping a long branch. "You want a treat?" Ruke didn't even glance her way. "You need to come outside, buddy. It's for your own good." When silence pervaded the air, she sighed and stepped closer, feeling foolish with someone watching her. She'd always hated being the center of attention, especially in school, and performed poorly under such pressure. So, she took away the distraction and stepped inside the stall, out of Caster's sight and only feet away from Ruke.

Craning her neck, Evangeline scanned her hazel eyes from hoof to head. He really was a magnificently beautiful creature, with deep brown spots that dotted tanned fur in a puzzle of perfection. His long legs were lean but strong, leading up to a thick body that boasted his full height. She'd always loved the look of their long necks, with that ridge of coarse fur sticking up like a mohawk. His head was huge compared to her measly human form, with a strong and defined jaw, pronounced ridge along the nose, and hooded brown eyes.

And right now, those eyes were filled with stubbornness.

"Look, I know it sucks. You lost someone you love and you're sad. You want everyone to leave you alone and just let you think about stuff. But you can't. You have to live and be with the other giraffes, because people are worried about you and vets who don't understand what it's like to be sad get the wrong idea. So, get your adorable stubborn butt out there." She offered him an insistent expression that was as silly as it was demanding and lifted the branch again, but Ruke only stomped a hoof. Evangeline responded with a stomp of her own, matching his stubbornness move for move. "I said, get a move on, you goof. Move!"

The word came out with more force than she intended, and the arm she threw out at her side, pointing to the pasture, surprised her even more. The gesture startled Ruke, who shifted and lifted his head high. But, to her delight, he turned and moved toward the open door.

"There you go," Evangeline said, her tone softer this time. "Good b—*umph*," she grunted and stepped back when Ruke flicked his tail her direction as he passed, giving her a mouthful of tail hair that she could only guess was the equivalent of a middle finger in response to her order.

In the privacy of the stall, Evangeline grinned. The smile stretched from ear to ear, even when she bit down on her bottom lip in an attempt to suppress it. The moment couldn't be contained, no matter what had happened in the past, despite how sad she'd been earlier that day. She'd done it, she'd accomplished something that helped another.

Maybe she wasn't as lost as she thought. Maybe, just maybe, her life could have meaning again.

CAUSE FOR CELEBRATION

SHE WATCHED RUKE for hours, eyes shining in the sunlight as they took in the sight of her favorite animal at the preserve. Ruke wandered around the pasture as though seeing it for the first time, tasting leaves, kicking at the grass, and even nudging Lady Regal with his long neck when he came to a stop beside her. Caster let her enjoy the time alone, working around her in the barn and never ordering her to help. He seemed to understand her need to be part of this moment, when she accomplished something no one else could, when she realized she was needed.

Now she sat at the small desk in her room, head braced up by one hand and pen grasped in the other. Her tutor was relentless in schoolwork, demanding a quiz every week, an essay every two weeks, and an evaluation every month. Her first couple evaluations had been completed and she assumed she passed, since she was allowed to stay at the preserve. Her second was only a few days away and she needed to ensure she'd read all the books and finished every assignment.

Otherwise, they'd make her go back.

Evangeline didn't have the luxury of a computer and wouldn't ask Jett to use his, not after everything he'd already done for her. So instead she suffered in silence at her desk, fingers and hand spasming each time she pressed pen to paper. Even before the accident she'd hated writing by hand — after all, she'd grown up in the technology era and was a typing and texting whiz. Putting pen to paper was a lost art that she used to turn her nose up at. Breaking her hand deepened that disdain, encouraging her to stick her tongue out at the pen and call it a few choice names in her head.

A knock at the door had her sitting back, grateful for the interruption despite knowing she was behind. The door opened slowly and Jett peeked in. "Am I interrupting?"

"No." She set her papers aside and sat up straighter. "Just schoolwork."

"Yup, that's why I'm here. Your tutor just called to say he's sick, so I'm filling in for the night." Jett set down a stack of books and glanced at it reproachfully, scratching at his beard. "I hope you're good at math, because I'm not."

"I'll teach you," she said with a ghost of a smile.

"Good." He handed her a folder. "Today's assignment. I'll take whatever ya have for the past couple days and make sure the tutor gets it." They swapped folders before Jett sat in the other chair and opened a book. "Answer these equations and we'll get to it. If ya need any help, I'll pretend to be a genius."

Jett observed the girl carefully as she took the book from him, noting the weary resolve in her eyes and the frown that creased her mouth. He'd noticed the expression several times in the past few weeks, recognized it from his many years helping Lettie with her arthritis pain, but was hesitant to speak his concerns for fear of being wrong. Or worse, insulting her and causing the girl to close herself off again after they'd made so much progress the last couple months.

But when her jaw clenched as she picked up the pen again, he knew he was right and that something had to be said.

"So you are in pain," he stated, lifting a brow when she glanced up, wariness in those all-seeing hazel eyes. "How long has your hand been bothering you?"

Evangeline drew back, her hand falling to her lap. "It always bothers me," she replied quietly.

"Why didn't you tell anyone?"

"There's nothing you can do."

"I can call the doctor and get you a prescription if you need it. I can get Caster to massage your hand. I can make sure you don't lift anything heavy with that hand," Jett rattled off the list. "Did you really think we wouldn't do anything if you asked?" When her eyes lowered to the desk and shoulders slumped ever so slightly, he knew his question was affirmed. "Did your mother not do anything?"

The question struck her hard, bringing back words she'd tried to forget.

It's just a hand. You got another one, don't you?

144

So you can't paint anymore. Don't be so selfish. Your father can't live anymore. You win.

It hurts so you'll never forget what you did.

I wish it had been you, not him.

"Evangeline?"

She took in a slow, deep breath, spreading her palms over the desk as though bracing herself. Her movements were slow, deliberate. "I did this to myself."

"By purposely getting into a car accident?" Jett stifled a sigh when she didn't reply. He wanted her to talk about the accident, vent about it, cry about it, whatever she needed to do to heal. But when it became clear she was closing off, he tried a different approach. "Well, just make sure you take it easy the next few days. No carrying buckets, no climbing up rocks to jump into the water."

Jett grinned when she looked up, surprise in her expression. "What? You really think I don't know where all my keepers go for hours at a time when they think I'm not looking?"

Evangeline hid a grin. "Then why do you let them?"

He shrugged. "They get their work done and they do it well. I figure it's good to let them think they got one over on the ole' boss. Just don't tell 'em I know, and I won't tell anyone you were in the giraffe enclosure." Jett laughed at the alarm in her eyes. "Like I said, I know everything. But I'm proud of ya. You did something none of us could. I thank you for that. I only hope now he'll keep letting you work with him."

Excitement lit a warm flame in her soul. "I can keep working with Ruke?"

"Of course. So long as you get to your homework."

At his pointed glance, Evangeline picked up the pen,

this time not even feeling the pain as she completed the assignment.

JETT LEANED BACK and stretched, eyeing Evangeline conspicuously. She was hunched over the math book, head braced, lips pressed together as she wrote out equations and pretended like it didn't hurt to do so. She was a stickler for appearing tough, Jett noticed, despite the fact that everyone had seen her break down. Part of him wondered if she needed to maintain the façade so people wouldn't think she was still the girl who came close to death by her own hands.

He had a feeling she was punishing herself for the accident that took her father's life, but couldn't quite figure out why. It went back to her mother, he was sure, but no one could quite figure out what. Rick, with all his years' experience as a caseworker, had his suspicions, as did Jett.

Rick suspected Evangeline was internalizing the guilt because of both her father's death and her mother's grief. He suspected Edith Frost's indifference and recently developed alcoholism had become a kind of burden for the teenager, who was trying to cope with the loss of both parents.

Jett had a more direct assumption. He may not have known Evangeline quite as long or been part of her counseling at the hospital, but he wasn't blind. There was no question in his mind that Edith had said something that set the girl off. He'd only known Evangeline for two months, but he saw that quiet strength within her. She could deal with more than she knew, more than anyone gave her credit for, but words were what hurt her. It had been after that phone call with her mother that Evangeline had her meltdown. No, the girl wasn't internalizing guilt. She was being flat-out blamed for her father's death.

"Let's get a snack," Jett announced, rising from the rickety wooden chair. "Math makes me hungry."

Evangeline frowned, glancing down at her notebook. "I'm not finished."

"You only have two left. You need to refuel to make sure you get them right. Come on." He gestured for her to follow while hiding a grin when she bit back a sigh and rose, clearly annoyed by the disruption but too polite to say so. Together they left the bunk and headed for the big house. "Whatcha hungry for?"

"I'm not really hungry," she admitted, following only because she was too nervous to do otherwise. The others may ignore his rules, but she was a stickler.

"You need to eat. We work you hard on the preserve." Jett dismissed her words just as easily as he walked across the yard. She bit back an argument and fell into step behind him, silently protesting in her own stubborn way. If he sensed her annoyance, he didn't comment, instead pulling open the door to the main house and gesturing for her to enter.

Evangeline stepped inside, frowning at the darkness. The house was usually lit up on the first floor, even throughout the night, since there were a lot of people who stayed on the grounds who enjoyed a late-night treat.

"Whatcha waiting for?" Jett asked as he passed Evangeline, who had stopped just inside the doorway. "Food ain't gonna come to you."

"But …" Seeing no good reason not to follow, she resigned herself to a walk through the dark, not knowing where the light switches were. When Jett pushed open the kitchen door, she peered into the shadows and frowned. "What's going on with the—"

"Happy birthday!"

Evangeline halted at the chorus of voices that assaulted her ears, eyes squinting in the sudden light that flooded the room. When her vision cleared, she saw the kitchen was packed with everyone who worked at the preserve, Lettie holding a cake, Caster at her side with a wide grin, Derek on her other with Bilbo on his shoulders. The others she knew more by face than name, but they all smiled back at her.

Jett clapped her on the shoulder. "Didn't think we'd forget, did ya?" he asked, laughter in his voice. "Birthdays are a big deal 'round here. Everyone in the gang gets a cake!"

She looked around the room, at all the smiling faces, at Lettie frantically lighting the candles, at the balloons and streamers hanging from the rafters. A sob caught in her throat, tears filling her eyes at the sight of so many people — so many strangers, essentially — who were there to celebrate her birthday. Even her own mother had forgotten, or at the very least, not wanted to acknowledge the day she gave birth to the girl who would later break her heart.

Lettie, seeing the tears in the girl's eyes, all but shoved the cake in front of Evangeline's face before they could fall. The cake was decorated with giraffe-patterned icing and little giraffe and goat figures playing in a green-icing pasture. "You best be blowing these out and making

148

a wish! We've got some hungry boys who want cake! If they get any closer you might end up with slobber icing."

Evangeline smiled, the grin lighting her face just as much as the flickering candlelight did. "I prefer my cakes slobber free," she said, then leaned over and blew out seventeen candles to the sound of cheers.

I wish for a life I can be proud of. A simple wish, not so simply achieved.

Activity blurred around her then, Lettie cutting the cake and handing her the first piece, the others crowding around for their own slice. Chairs scraped against the floor as everyone found their seats, reminiscing over birthdays celebrated that year and further in the past.

"Remember Lettie's fortieth? Jett set the kitchen on fire trying to make an *ice cream* cake!" Caster laughed out, earning a smirk from Jett.

"Ah, but it's the thought that counts," Lettie replied, planting a kiss on her husband's cheek. "And who are you to talk, Lancaster? *You* mixed up salt and sugar for what I'm pretty sure is the only Kindred Hides cake that even the goats wouldn't eat."

Evangeline couldn't help the snort that escaped, though she tried to hide it by wiping her mouth with a napkin. Caster raised a brow at her. "Oh, you think it's funny? Well what if I—"

"Okay, listen up!" Jett said loudly as he stood, having known what was about to happen. "As the undeniably amazing owner of the preserve, I hereby declare that I get the honor of giving Miss Evangeline here her first birthday gift."

Her attention shot to Jett, head snapping to catch his gaze. "Gift? You didn't have to—"

"I know," he cut in. "Gifts have nothing to do with *have* to, and everything to do with *want* to." He handed her a wrapped present the size of a shoebox. "This is from me and Lettie."

Tenderly, almost hesitantly, Evangeline unwrapped the box. Nerves twisted in her stomach at the worry of them spending money on her. Those nerves turned into humor when she saw the giraffe bobblehead sitting in the box. She picked it up and shook it, the head bouncing to the beat of everyone's laughter.

"Because every giraffe whisperer needs a giraffe bobblehead, obviously," Jett said from his end of the table.

Evangeline grinned. "Of course. I'm going to name him Jett." Lettie let out a hoot and clapped her husband on the back as others did the same.

"Okay, my turn." Caster handed her a bag with about fifteen pieces of tissue paper. "Wrapped it myself."

"Obviously," Lettie said as Evangeline pulled out piece after piece until finally she pulled out a rock the size of her palm. "What on earth is that for?" Lettie asked for the girl.

"I chipped it off PJ's rock," Caster replied proudly. "Now you and PJ can battle for the title."

Evangeline closed her fingers around the rock, her grin widening as she remembered that day. "I think we both know whose boss. And it ain't me."

Lana, a keeper for the big cats, handed her a long, paper-thin package and crossed her arms with a wry expression. "So you'll always know who's who. Hang it over your bed or something."

Curious, Evangeline unwrapped the item, then chuckled when she saw what was screen-printed on a banner:

Cheetahs have spots. Leopards have open spots. Jaguars have spots in spots. "I won't make that mistake again," she promised with a grin, thinking back to the day she'd almost walked in an occupied jaguar enclosure thinking it was the empty leopard preserve.

Derek slid her a box after that, winking in her direction. "Bilbo wants ya ta have it."

Shooting him a suspicious glance, she unwrapped the box and lifted the top, confusion crossing her features as she pulled out a hunk of metal. "What is it?"

"Hey!" Caster protested. "That's my belt buckle!"

"Mine now," Evangeline said while the others cracked up. Caster pointed at her again, a silent but friendly challenge, when she clutched the buckle to her chest.

And so the gifts went, one gag after the next, each personalized in some way. From Tatiana, a piece of lettuce to feed Ruke. From Lettie, a framed picture of PJ. It amazed her that everyone cared enough to not only be with her on her birthday, but actually give her gifts that meant something, even if they were gags. After everything had been unwrapped and laughed at accordingly, they all got to finishing their cake while rejoicing in the night.

Celebration rang out around her, a group of men and women so comfortable with one another that they had become family. They smiled genuine smiles, laughed hearty laughs, hugged and touched and joked in ways that she longed to understand. Watching them in this moment, she could almost feel the things she once thought she deserved.

Love.

Happiness.

Family.

Life.

I wish it had been you, not him.

Her mother's voice filled her head — just as a splatter of cake smacked her upside it.

Evangeline jumped, lifting a hand to her cheek, fingers coming back a mix of brown and green. Her eyes traveled down the table, which had gone silent. All attention was on her, eyes wide, expressions a mix of surprise and humor.

Finally, her gaze caught Caster, who was staring at her with that annoying lifted brow, a silent challenge. She wiped a hand down her face, cupping the icing as she rose from her chair, her face a portrait of irritation and wounded insult. She pushed away from the table and stalked toward the door.

When she passed Caster, who had lowered his eyes to the table reproachfully, she turned quickly and smeared the icing in her hand across his face. Hoots and hollers exploded from around the table, and just as Lettie held up her hands to stop the oncoming war, everyone else joined in.

Cake flew across the table, icing slicking the floors, coloring hair, staining clothes. Icing-covered hands found exposed faces, some launching pieces of cake from one end of the table to the other. Derek sputtered when even Bilbo got in on the action, poking at his human's face with a handful of icing then leaping on the chandelier to escape revenge, nibbling on a piece of cake as his wide round eyes took in the scene below him. The sounds of cake hitting window and wood echoed throughout the kitchen, sneakers squeaking on icing, shouted words and laughter muffled by layers of dessert.

Lettie rose up to her full height, ready to shout at

them all, but paused when Jett put a hand on her shoulder. "Look," he whispered from their safe corner of the kitchen. Lettie followed his gaze, frown curling up into a smile when she saw Evangeline trapped around the waist by Caster's arms as Janet, a maintenance worker, smeared cake in her face and Bilbo hopped on her shoulder from the chandelier, picking icing out of her hair.

And all the while, the girl laughed.

21

A BRUSH OF FAITH

EVANGELINE STUMBLED OUT of the main house, body racking with giggles as she wiped at her arms and face. Jett had given her a towel, but only a long, hot shower would clean her now.

"I should help," she managed to protest before he closed the door behind her. "I helped make the mess."

"You'll do no such thing," he replied. "It's your birthday and birthday girls don't do cleanup. Now git."

She opened her mouth to argue, then stopped when Caster was shoved out the door behind her. He grinned at her sheepishly and held out an arm. "Walk you to your room, m'lady?"

Still in a giddy mood from the cake fight, Evangeline took his arm and allowed him to walk her the short distance to her bunk. Once there, he leaned against the railing and reached back, producing a wrapped box that was tucked into his waistband.

"So, gag gifts are the tradition for birthdays, but I thought I'd get you something you could actually use."

Evangeline took the box, eyeing him warily. "Why?"

"Because I wanted to. Now don't be stubborn. Open it."

She half expected a snake to pop out when she opened the lid. What she found instead took her breath away.

"Caster," she breathed quietly, running her fingers over the four wooden brushes, each a different size, each a white-bristled brush for a true painter. She longed to pick one up, run a stroke through the air, remember what it felt like to be an artist again. The fact that he remembered such a small detail from a conversation so long ago tugged at her heart, chipping away at its barrier.

"Caster," she said again around the tears, "these are amazing. Like, top-of-the-line stuff. But … I can't use them. I told you, I—"

"You got a gimpy hand," he said, grinning when she glared up at him. "What? It's the truth, ain't it? Here, gimme." He held out a hand until she relented and gave her own. "Birthday hand massage," he said. "Lettie's orders."

She doubted that, but let him massage her hand because no matter the reason why, he knew what he was doing. Even though certain parts of her hand were tender, sometimes painful when touched, his massages did make her hand feel better.

He watched her face as he worked, noting the grimaces when he hit a particularly sensitive spot. But she hadn't told him to stop, so he figured he was doing something right. "So, you like it here?" he asked, the quiet starting to eat at his nerves.

"Yes," she answered honestly. "I've always loved animals. It's pretty amazing being here."

"You ever think about going home?"

Her breath caught as she considered the question. Very carefully, she answered, "I think about my mother. But … she doesn't think about me."

He heard the plea in her response, the desire for someone, anyone, to ask in this moment what was wrong. "Why do you say that?"

"You celebrated my birthday," Evangeline replied, looking up and almost chuckling at the green icing coating his dark brown hair. She guessed she looked close to the same. "She ... forgot. Said she didn't have time for me."

"Why would she say that?"

"Because I killed my father."

The words were said so sadly, with such matter-of-fact resolution, that Caster dropped her hand and lifted her chin so their eyes met. "Now I know that's a load of crap. Jett told me about the accident. It was just that, an accident."

She shrugged, all merriment from the cake fight wearing off. "It doesn't matter anyway."

"It does matter," he challenged, anger rising in his voice. Anger for her mother. Anger for the fact that she believed what she said. Anger for not being able to convince her otherwise. "It matters because you're still punishing yourself for an *accident*."

"What do you know?" she spat back. "You weren't

there. You don't understand."

"So make me understand."

They stared at one another for a moment, each refusing to back down in the silent challenge. Finally Caster relented with a sigh. "You're not alone anymore, Evangeline. Just know that much. You've got everyone here, Jett, Lettie, the whole gang, whether you want to believe it or not. And I really hope you try painting again. If you truly love it, then don't let a little pain stop you from doing the things you love most."

He left her standing there, one hand still outstretched, the other clutching the box of brushes.

22

THE CRUELTY OF FATE

"SOMEONE WANTS TO ask you a question."

"Please, Dad." She rolled her eyes, sparing him a moment's glance. *"It's not like that."*

"Nope. Father knows best."

"Don't think so."

"I think it's sweet. My little elf and the boy whose legs I'll have to break if he breaks your heart."

"Dad! He can hear you!" She huffed, annoyance clear in her tone. *"Since when do you care about my love life anyway?"*

"I'm your dad. I always care."

"How convenient."

"Wake up."

She glanced over at her father, who sat in the passen-

ger seat. Urgency filled his face. "What?"

He reached out and shook her shoulder hard. "Wake up. Evangeline, wake up!"

"Evangeline! Wake up!"

Confusion filled her thoughts as her eyes opened to sunlight. That confusion only settled deeper when she saw Janet leaning over her, shaking her shoulders. The woman's blue eyes were red, her lips pressed together tightly. "What's going on?"

"It's PJ. Something's happening in the goat pen. Jett said to get you out there asap."

Bewilderment mixed with panic as Evangeline followed Janet out the door, barely stopping to pull on a pair of jeans and her boots. Her tank top she'd slept in would have to do for now. It was only a five-minute walk from the big house to the goat pen; she made the run in two.

Lettie stood outside the pen, gripping the fence with white fingers and knuckles. On the inside kneeled Jett, Caster, and Donnie, one of the part-time keepers and full-time med staff.

"What is it?" Evangeline asked as she skidded to a stop by Lettie. Her knee protested at the movement, but she brushed off the pain and craned her neck to see over the fence, gasping when she saw one of the goats collapsed on the gravel. "Is that …?"

But she knew. Only one goat had fur black as night from head to hoof.

Her words, her tears, caught in her throat as she entered the pen, fear slowing her steps. Her heart ached the closer she got, lungs shuddering with each intake of air. But still she moved forward until she reached the three men, dropping to her knees next to them.

"PJ."

Jett glanced to his right at the girl, eyes red. "He's not gone yet, Evangeline. That's why I called you out here. You two, you got something special. I wanted him to see you one last time."

She reached out a trembling hand, fingers grazing over soft fur, eyes latched on to PJ's. The goat, the ornery creature that knocked her off his rock yet let her pet him through the fence, stared up at her. She'd never claimed to be one with animals, but in that moment she swore she saw something close to happiness that she was there, petting him, comforting him.

"What happened?"

"Seizure, we think," Donnie replied. "Not sure what else just yet. Caster found him just a bit ago like this."

She didn't look at Caster, couldn't. Not when PJ still held her gaze as though pleading for her undivided attention. Giving him just that, she lay down and stretched out next to him on the gravel. He remained motionless, but watched her every move, his sides quivering and his mouth trembling uncontrollably. They lay side by side, his hooves pressed against her stomach, her hands stroking his side, his face, his neck. Gentle caresses that told the animal just how loved he was by the girl who'd known him but months.

"Hey, buddy," Evangeline whispered, her voice quivering. "It's okay." Somewhere behind her she heard Caster sniffling. "You helped me out a lot when I got here, you know that?" She stroked a finger down the goat's nose, scratched under his chin. PJ blinked once, gaze never leaving her. "When I saw you I knew I could make it here.

You helped make everything okay. And I'm here now for you, to make it all okay. I love you, little guy."

As if waiting for her declaration, PJ breathed his final breath.

SHE SAT, UNMOVING, on the rock inside the goat pen. PJ's rock.

For how long, Evangeline didn't know. Donnie had long ago removed the goat's body from the pen and the others had gone about their day, albeit solemnly and with lowered gazes. Lettie retreated to the big house, Caster following. Now only Jett remained, watching her from a small distance, making sure she would survive this loss. He hated to see her in pain, this child who was quickly cementing a place in his heart despite the fact that she would one day leave his preserve. He knew the arrangement was temporary, he and Lettie only fostering the girl during her time in the program, but Jett already cared for her like his own.

When he couldn't stand her silence any longer, he approached, taking a seat next to the girl who had seen too much death.

"PJ was a grumpy little guy," Jett began, drawing up his knees. "Never got along with anyone. Then you came along. Made him the happiest little brat at the preserve." He chuckled, but Evangeline didn't even crack a smile. Jett sighed. "It's okay to be sad, Evangeline. It's okay to be angry, even."

"It's okay," she repeated, her voice strangely distant.

The joy leftover from her birthday party five days ago had vanished with PJ's dying breath. "It's okay to be sad. It's okay to be angry. It's okay to feel bad. It's okay to not talk. It's okay, it's okay, it's okay. You know what they never tell you?" She turned her hazel eyes to Jett, who reeled back at the steely glare. "That's it's okay to wish you could join him."

Jett took in a breath, knowing they were no longer talking about PJ. He remained silent while she continued in that quiet, far-off voice.

"Cry, pray, mourn … get over it. Everyone dies. You don't get to mourn when you're the reason he died."

"You don't believe that," he said before realizing he interrupted. "Evangeline?"

"I was driving," she whispered. "I must be held accountable."

"By who? Your mother?" Her back stiffened, mouth pressing together in a thin line. Jett cursed inwardly but nudged her shoulder with his own in hopes of softening the tension in the air. "I want you to know, little elf, that no one will hold you accountable here."

Her head snapped his direction, frown turning into a look of surprise. "What did you just say?"

Jett's brow furrowed. "Only that no one—"

"No. You called me little elf. Why?"

Jett lifted a shoulder. "I saw your file. It's your initials, no? Evangeline Lorelei Frost. I just thought it was cute. I didn't mean to offend ya."

"You didn't." She turned her gaze back to the goat pen, the furry bodies wandering around as though searching for their fallen friend, as she rested her head on her knees. "My father used to call me that, is all."

They remained there, silent sentries, for another hour. When Jett lifted himself from the ground and offered Evangeline a hand, she accepted.

23

FROM THE PAST

DIRT SHOWERED THE porch floor, boots knocked against wood. The steady *thud thud thud* echoed throughout the big house, reaching Lettie's ears as she waited patiently by the phone.

"Phone call," she told Evangeline when the girl entered. "Sounds like a young man." Lettie grinned, but the smile wasn't returned.

Evangeline took the phone, having no idea what young man would want to call her. "Hello?"

"Miss me?"

"Cam." Now she did smile, the sound of a familiar voice from home filling her with warmth. "What's up? How did you get this number?"

"That guy Rick gave it to me before you left, that day

I met him at the hospital when you were discharged. I wanted to call and say happy birthday. I know I'm late, but the parents took away my cell. Flunked a test. You know how they are."

She did. She knew they were crafty and thought up punishments that fit the crime. Few things did Cam love more than his smartphone, which made losing it for bad grades all the more painful. "Sucks about the phone. Guess you better start studying after school instead of taking your marathon naps."

"Not likely," he replied. "So how was the birthday?"

"It was pretty good. They made me a cake here and got me a bunch of gag gifts." She didn't tell him about the brushes. That seemed too personal, too breakable.

"Sound like good people way out there in hippie land. You get to work with any cool animals?"

"Yeah." Briefly she told him about some of the work she'd done, leaving out a few details about Ruke and all about PJ. She couldn't talk about that yet; it had only been a week and she wasn't ready. He chuckled at her stories about Bilbo, and she found herself missing that familiar chuckle, laughing with her only real friend.

The feeling was short lived, however, after his next words.

"So ... I saw your mom at the store the other day. She's ... not the same person she used to be." When Evangeline only huffed in acknowledgement, he continued. "I thought she'd at least smile or something. I said hi, asked if she'd heard from you and how you were."

When he fell silent, Evangeline pressed him for more, hating herself for wanting to know. "What did she say? Cam, what did she say?" she repeated when he didn't answer.

"She said … She said she doesn't talk to murderers."

Murderers.

One word, a simple word really. One word that took her back to the day that told her she lost not only her father, but her mother too.

She sat on the edge of her hospital bed, ready to go home. While she waited she stared out the window overlooking a small manmade pond, where a flock of geese swam in its center. The bright morning sun should have calmed and comforted the girl, inspired a smile that soon she would be free of this suffocating hospital room and in the fresh air. But still the pain remained. Her wounds were healing, though her heart remained broken.

Her mother was late. An hour late, to be exact. Only when the nurses called for the fifth time did Edith finally show up and order her daughter to the car.

Panic set in at the thought of being in a vehicle. Just outside the hospital doors, Evangeline clutched her jacket, fighting back nerves as she leaned against a bench to support her aching right knee. At her mother's sharp bark she pushed herself forward. Sheer terror caused her hands to shake as she opened the back door, bile rising in her throat as she settled down on the seat and drew the seatbelt across her body. They rode home in silence, and when they arrived, Edith left Evangeline to find her way inside alone.

The girl opened the car door slowly, getting out even slower. It was hard to move with her knee in a brace and arm in a sling. The doctors said it would take a while for the rest of her body to heal just from the shock of the accident. She realized just how right they were when it took her at least five minutes to limp the short distance from the car to the front door.

She found her mother in the living room, glass of wine already in hand. "Mom, I just wanted to say ... I'm sorry. I don't know what else to say or do, but ... I hope that one day you can forgive me."

"Forgive you?" Edith's stare was filled with malice when she directed it at her daughter. "You were driving. You were on the phone. You were distracted. You killed your father."

A tear rolled down her cheek, a single tear after so many already shed. "I know. And I'm—"

"Sorry?" Edith cut in with a scoff. "Does that bring him back? Does that make it all better?"

"... No."

"Damn right, no." Edith turned her eyes to the television after refilling her wine glass. "I'm supposed to forgive a murderer."

It was quiet, said just beneath her breath, but Evangeline heard the words as though they rang right next to her ears.

Murderer.

You killed your father.

Murderer.

"Evie?"

Evangeline snapped back to the phone call, surprised by the tears in her eyes. She didn't want to cry over Edith Frost anymore, but part of her heart still longed for her mother's affections. "Yeah."

"So what do you think?"

"About what?"

Cam sighed into the phone. "About telling the truth.

If your mom knew—"

"No."

"But, Evie. It's all been a lie. If she knew—"

"No."

"She wouldn't hate you," he finished. "I almost told her, Evie. Hearing what she said about you, I almost snapped and called her a few things that would probably make you not wanna be my friend anymore. But she would have deserved it. She needs to hear what happened. And I swear to God, if you don't tell her the truth soon, then I will."

"Are you threatening me?" Evangeline snapped, a headache brewing. "Let her think what she wants. Let her hate me. It's better for her."

"What about what's better for you? Or for me?" he asked. "I have to live with this too, Evie. You think it's easy for me?"

She slumped against the wall, defeated. "I guess I hadn't thought about it like that."

"Well, think about it. The parents are telling me to get off the phone. I'll give you a call in a week or so, catch up then. And I'm serious, Evie. Enough is enough."

ENOUGH IS ENOUGH.

Cam's words echoed through her mind, cementing in her consciousness with each step she took toward the giraffe enclosure. He was right, but that didn't make it any easier. Telling the truth of what happened the day of the accident would only make life better for herself, and maybe for Cam. The truth would be Evangeline's redemption, but her mother needed to believe the lie. It was what made her father's death bearable, as bearable as any death could be.

Ruke was in the yard, standing close to the barn. She could tell he wanted to go back inside, but someone had closed off the entrance, forcing him to remain out in the great outdoors. The other giraffes, Lady Regal included, wandered around the enclosure, stopping to chew on leaves here and there.

Evangeline walked around the side of the enclosure where the ground rose up in a grassy hill. At that spot, the enclosure fence was also lowered enough to allow the giraffes contact with anyone on the outside. Ruke followed her to the opening, animal and human walking on opposite sides of the fence, each silently pondering secret thoughts. The quiet stretched between them, filled only by the call of birds in the distance and the steady hum of a tractor's engine three enclosures over. When they finally came to a stop, the fence reached up to Ruke's chest and Evangeline's waist.

"Hey, boy," she said quietly as she approached, holding up a handful of alfalfa hay. "Got your favorite." A smile flickered across her face when he leaned over and tugged the hay from her fingers. His long tongue wrapped around her wrist, leaving behind a trail of thick, sticky saliva. "Thanks," she laughed.

"There's that laugh. Haven't heard it for a few days."

Evangeline turned to see Caster approaching. Her smile twisted into a smirk. "Hasn't been a reason to."

"Nah, there's always a reason to laugh. Just gotta find it." He grinned up at Ruke. "He seems better, huh?" She nodded. "So, I was thinking. Jett told me to repaint the outside of the goat pen like three months ago. I hate painting, so it hasn't been done yet."

"Okay." She eyed him curiously.

"Well, I still don't want to paint it. But, I mean, it's really a great wall. Lots of space, great sunlight all around it, nice view of the preserve. Probably be pretty fun to—"

"You trying to Tom Sawyer me into painting a wall for you?"

Caster chuckled. "Something like that. But I was thinking maybe you could paint a mural. A kind of memorial for PJ, you know?"

"Oh." Her eyes turned to the ground. She was both thrilled and saddened by the request. "You know I can't paint anymore."

"Have you tried?" he challenged. "Tell you what. You paint, and I'll massage out any pain. Now, that's a good deal, if I do say so myself."

Evangeline huffed. "You just don't want to paint."

"Well, that's true."

"I'll think about it."

PUSH THROUGH

SHE WAITED UNTIL the preserve was silent, only late-night animal calls to be heard from her bedroom window. Even after the moon had risen and hours passed since the last bunkhouse light flicked off, still Evangeline sat at her desk staring at the box of brushes. It had been untouched since her birthday celebration, out of fear or respect she wasn't sure.

Almost hesitantly, she reached out and stroked a finger down one of the brushes, a specialty fan blender brush with white bristles that arced out in a wave. Next to it sat a broader glazing brush, the handle wider, the bristles clumped together. Two very different types of brushes for two very different types of strokes for one beautiful painting.

And the only artist able to wield them.

She set a determined pace as she stalked around the bunkhouses and to the goat pen, dim flashlight in one hand and brushes in the other. She was startled to see the wall was covered with a cloth, and recently washed, she realized after lifting the fabric. A few trays of paints along with a jar of mineral spirits were already waiting for her outside the pen, as though Caster had known she'd come when no one was looking. It almost annoyed her that he thought he knew her and her art so well.

Almost.

Evangeline sat on the soft grass, crossing her legs and setting the flashlight next to her after adjusting the brightness. It wasn't the greatest light to work by, but it was the best she could do at night without waking anyone. But she wasn't worried — she'd spent her entire life with a brush in hand and could mix colors with her eyes closed.

Paint me a picture, my little elf.

Her father's words met her ears as though whispered on the wind. She smiled, having forgotten until this moment that moment of serenity amidst chaos, one last second of lucidity before the world turned black. A terrible moment, and yet, one that reminded her of the bond she once shared with her father.

Unconditional love.

Unquestioning faith.

A lifetime of happy memories.

The brush felt both awkward and natural in her hand, fitting comfortably between her fingers. It was second nature, holding a brush, turning it into an extension of her arm that moved as naturally as any other part of her. Her passion hadn't faded, and neither had the seamless way in which she moved. A twinge of pain spiked up her middle finger when she dipped the brush in white paint and dragged it across the wall, but she ignored it. Just as she ignored the constant ache that traveled up to her elbow with each stroke.

Pain was fleeting.

CASTER CHUCKLED AS he approached the goat pen. The morning was early still, the sun barely peeking above the horizon. Only a few of the others were awake, having headed to the cabin for breakfast. He'd been on his way too, only to be diverted by Jett when he was asked to find the Frost gal. Caster had his suspicions as to where she might be, and was eager to see if he was correct.

He saw her feet first, bare feet covered with dirt. His eyes traveled from her feet to the rest of her, seeing Evangeline lying on her side on the grass in a pair of loose jeans and tank top, using one arm as a pillow as she slept. Her hands, arms, and cheeks were flecked with color, an amusing mix of grays, reds, blues, and greens.

Next to her sat her brushes, clean and propped up in an empty cup that he assumed had held her choice of beverage the night before. The paint trays were closed next to the brushes. After glancing over the supplies, Caster finally looked at the wall.

It was beautiful. Unfinished, but beautiful.

She'd started with the trees in the background, some only partially outlined with light brown strokes, others fully painted in shades of vibrant greens. They soared into a cloudless blue sky brightened by an afternoon sun. Below those trees stretched a pasture spotted with wildflowers of all colors. And all around that pasture were goats. He saw Chadster the showgoat standing proudly by a gorgeous red flower clearly meant to be as arrogant as the animal. He saw PJ, or what had been painted of him so far, atop his rock in the center of the pasture. Off to the side were outlines of people, children and adults watching the goats play.

Kneeling down, Caster gently shook Evangeline's shoulder. "Rise and shine." He smiled when she rose, glancing around in surprise. "I'm guessing you meant to slip back to your room at some point."

"Um ... yeah." Evangeline sat up and rubbed her eyes.

"Why did you come out here and paint in the middle of the night? I'm sure Jett and Lettie would have given you a couple days off to paint this."

She lifted a shoulder, the truth embarrassing her more than the fact that she'd fallen asleep outside. "I don't like people watching me when I paint. It makes me nervous, and then I mess up."

Caster gave the painting an appreciative onceover. "You got skills, girl. I don't think anyone could mess you up. But anyway, how's your hand?"

She looked down at her right hand, not surprised to see her fingers curled at the middle knuckles. A dull stabbing pain pulsed in her palm. "Hurts."

"Well, a promise is a promise." Caster sat on the dew-dropped grass next to her and took her hand, massaging from the palm outward. His thumbs pressed into tender spots but she didn't make him stop, instead biting her bottom lip through the pain and nearly sighing in relief when her fingers began to uncurl. "I'm good, huh?" he asked when he saw that relief in her eyes.

"I suppose."

He chuckled to himself as he finished the massage, then helped her to her feet. "Come on. Jett sent me to fetch ya. Wants to talk about something. He's probably wondering where we are by now."

He brought her to the main cabin and into the office, where Jett sat at his desk with Rick. Steaming cups of coffee rested on the desk in front of them. Evangeline stopped in the doorway, wondering why the caseworker — social worker? She could never remember which — was there.

"Morning," Jett said with a nod. "Thanks, Caster. You can get to it now."

Caster, recognizing the dismissal, simply nodded and left, leaving Evangeline to remain.

"Good morning," Rick greeted, offering the girl a smile and wondering only briefly why smudges of color were all over her face and arms. He saw the hesitation in her eyes at his greeting. "How are you?"

"Is everything okay?" she asked. "Why are you here?"

"Just a checkup," he replied, keeping his tone calm to match her worried one. "I told you I'd be checking in randomly. I'll be here for a couple days to observe and make sure all is well."

"All *is* well," she said defensively, fearing that he had been sent to bring her back regardless of what he claimed.

Jett rose, taking his coffee with him. "I'll leave you two to it. Come find me when you're done, be with the rhinos today."

She remained in the doorway another few moments before relenting and taking a seat in the chair Jett had vacated, enjoying the fact that she sat across from Rick, separated by the desk. Taking in a deep breath and placing her hands on the scarred wood, Evangeline broke the silence. "So ... what do you want to know?"

Rick sat back and took a sip of coffee. "Tell me how things have been."

"Fine."

"Care to elaborate?"

She sighed, knowing the only way to end the conversation was to actually talk. "I really like it here, okay? These people are nice to me. They don't care about what happened and they treat me nice. They celebrated my birthday."

"And what about the work?"

"It's hard work, but I enjoy it." Evangeline shrugged. "I get to work with the goats and giraffes, and sometimes the others. They trust me. I mostly work with Caster. He shows me the ropes, makes sure I'm not screwing anything up. I'm exhausted at the end of the day, but it's worth it."

"Do you ever work with anyone else?"

Evangeline thought back to a few days ago. "Sometimes with Jett. The other day I worked with Tatiana when Caster had a day off and went into town or something. She mostly deals with everything plant related here."

"And how did that go?"

"Kinda boring at times, but whatever." The teenager shrugged, her words honest. She liked Tatiana, an older woman with shockingly white hair that contrasted bronzed skin, a thick accent that spoke of far-off origins, and so much plant knowledge that Evangeline's head still spun when she thought about preserve's prized specialist.

"Two different kinds of nature here," Tatiana had said while they worked on weeding out the vegetable garden. Evangeline hadn't responded to much she said, but Tatiana didn't let that deter her. *"You have the animals and you have the plants. Different as night and day, but all a part of nature. And we're in the middle of it all."*

"And what about the day a couple weeks ago, when you … acted out, shall we say?"

Evangeline sucked in a breath, having known that would come up but hoping it wouldn't all the same. "It was a moment of weakness. Someone said something, and I was already upset, and … There's no excuse. It was immature and I know it. I'm just glad they let me stay."

"Why were you upset?"

She glanced up to see Rick watching her with calming eyes. "Just … My mom forgot my birthday," she admitted, hating herself for doing so.

Rick watched her, watched some internal fight wrestling between her head and heart. It always came back to her mother, but still he couldn't figure out why. "Jett told me you called her. When you spoke to her, did she ask how you are doing? How your wounds are healing?"

"No."

"Do you mind if I ask now?"

"No."

"Then," Rick motioned to her hands, "do you mind if I see for myself?"

After a moment of hesitation, Evangeline offered her left hand, removing the bracelet she always wore that covered the ugly scar. She turned her eyes away when he took her wrist and observed the healed wound. He looked for only a few seconds, but they were enough for shame to creep into her heart.

Rick released her wrist, seeing the expression that told him what she thought of what she'd tried to do to herself. "Evangeline, I asked you this at the hospital, but I'm going to ask you again. Why did you do this?"

The desire, the need, to finally tell someone ached so badly she thought her heart would stop. But Rick wasn't the one to tell. He didn't know her, didn't understand the way she felt, the guilt she lived with, the lies she told everyone. And so she told him the only truth she knew.

"It should have been me, not him."

A TEST IS FAILED

CASTER EYED THE veterinarian, fighting the urge to clench his fists nervously. He'd known — they'd all known — that Dr. Bane would be back to check on Ruke, but today was not a good day.

They'd closed off the barn, not allowing any of the giraffes access inside until nightfall. This was done to keep Ruke outside, as the animal had a tendency to saunter back into the comfort of his stall as soon as the keepers' backs were turned. But Ruke wasn't exactly pleased with the new arrangement. If the giraffe could speak, Caster had a feeling he'd be putting Ruke in a timeout for foul language in the voice of a mopey teenager. The mental picture almost made him laugh before the vet's next question cut into his thoughts.

"You think this is normal?"

Caster bit back a sigh, along with a few choice words. "I never said that. I just said that we're doing our best."

Dr. Bane walked along the fence, peering through the chain links at Ruke, who was pressed up against the closed door of his stall, head braced against the metal as though attempting to push through the wall. "How long has he been like this?"

"I ... I don't know."

"I see." Dr. Bane wrote something on a notebook, his face a portrait of concern. "I want to do a physical on Ruke, see how he's progressing, then we'll discuss what to do next. It's also time for the elephant calf's evaluation. Did you give him a name yet?"

"Sterling," Caster answered absently. "He's in the barn today. We kept him in for the exam."

"Good." Dr. Bane turned away from the giraffes after sending a final frown at Ruke. He pointed over his shoulder with his pen. "We'll start with him."

RICK INSISTED ON a tour of the preserve, even though he'd seen it all several times before. He wanted to see Kindred Hides through Evangeline's eyes, get a feel for how she viewed the animals and her work. So he let her be his guide, going wherever she directed and making notes on her progress.

Just in the short time he'd been there, he could see the change in the girl. Evangeline was blossoming, whether she realized it or not. Her growth was a direct contrast to her mother's, which was nothing short of stagnant. Rick had met with Edith Frost just before flying out to California, offering grief counseling services to help her cope with the loss of her husband, but unlike Evangeline, the elder Frost wasn't yet interested in being happy again.

Because he knew that, Rick didn't mention the visit to Evangeline. He wanted her to focus on her own progress without having to worry about her mother.

"What's going on here?" he asked when they stopped just outside the elephant enclosure. On the other side, Caster stood with three other keepers, treating the elephants to an afternoon snack one by one while another older man stood back while observing a youngling.

"Oh, they are evaluating Sterling, the calf," Evangeline answered. "Just a checkup."

"What is the white … gate?"

"It's a weight thing," she said. "I forget the name. It kind of serves as a gate between the barn and the enclosure, but they use it for medical exams."

Rick peered through the cables, wondering at her response. He'd never seen the contraption in use before. The calf was secured between the bars, blocked on either end from entering or leaving, so the vet could reach through and perform the exam. "And how does it work?"

"Well, from what I understand, the bottom section is a scale so they can weigh the animal. Then they can close off the front and back if they need to do an exam. They can also squeeze the sides together and actually tilt the animal, so if they need to look at their legs or feet or stomach, the animal is off the ground and it's safer for everyone."

"Interesting."

And he meant it. Never having been one much for nature, everything about the preserve fascinated Rick and he enjoyed learning more — and especially enjoyed learning from Evangeline.

"You seem to know your way around," he commented, easing into his next line of questioning. "Getting comfortable here?"

"Yeah."

"Is it taking your mind off of things?"

Evangeline looked over at him briefly before turning her eyes back to Sterling, who was clearly unhappy being on the scale while the vet went through his exam. "Some days are better than others."

"Would you like to tell me about the bad days?"

"No."

Rick nodded, writing down another quick note. "Have you talked to anyone about that day?"

"No."

"Will you talk about it with me?"

"No."

She had closed off, he thought with a frown. Whatever joy she'd felt in showing him around had curdled. Rick took in a deep breath. "Alright then, let's continue the tour."

26

BREAK THE RULES

SHE WATCHED RICK leave, his rental car kicking up a trail of dust as he left the preserve behind. For one full week he watched her, studied her every move, insisted on daily talks that told him things she could only guess at. The steady *click-click* of his pen still echoed in her ears, reminding her that she was being watched, *why* she was being watched. And when he finally left, she could only hope he wouldn't force her to go with him.

Now that he was gone, she was to report in to Jett, find out her tasks for the day. She wanted to work, to get her mind off the observation, forget about why she was at the preserve and instead simply enjoy being there.

Inside the main cabin, Evangeline made her way to the office, stopping when she heard voices. She paused, wondering if she should knock, then lowered her raised fist when she heard Jett's agitated voice and the name *Ruke*. Against her better judgment, she took a cue from Caster, planted her feet, and listened.

On the other side of the door, Jett glared across his desk at the man who had come to visit — nay, *invade* — his preserve. The man was a spindly creature, tall and ghastly thin, thick black hair covering a large forehead and shadowing bright eyes. He wore a crisp suit despite the heat and shoes that likely cost more than any of the keepers' monthly salary.

The man was Robert Tindle. Inspector, advocate.

Enemy.

Jett blew out a breath. "I appreciate the concern, Mr. Tindle, but I assure you everything here is up to code and everyone here treats the animals with the utmost respect. I don't know who you've been talking to, but I can guess, and—"

"It doesn't matter who, Jett. You know this. All that matters is that the complaint was filed, and we must follow up with all such reports."

"Yeah, I know. And I also know this *person*, who I'm betting is named Ash, is simply upset that she is no longer with the preserve." Jett kept a close eye on the man, knowing he was right when he saw the way he pressed his lips together. "Our animals are well cared for. You've known me for twenty years, Robert. You know how well I care for them."

"I do know." Tindle nodded. "Which is why I am extending you the courtesy of this visit instead of issuing an official report. I spoke with your veterinarian, Jett. I read his own report of Ruke and the barn."

Jett's jaw clenched, dread dropping into the pit of his stomach. "That was … not what it seems, I assure you. We have done our best with Ruke, but he needs time. The vet saw only one moment out of months of rehabilitation and mourning."

"And that one moment indicated potentially severe complications for your preserve."

Defeated, Jett fell back against the hard wood of his office chair. "So what do you want to do?"

"I want to observe Ruke. Right now."

Just outside the door, Evangeline froze, eyes wide. He wanted to observe Ruke at that very moment. Ruke, who had been huddled inside the barn ever since Dr. Bane's visit eight days ago. Ruke, who had started to get better only to regress for reasons unknown. She knew this *Mr. Tindle* wouldn't understand the work they were doing, or why the giraffe was being so difficult.

Knowing what she had to do, Evangeline crept away from the door. When she reached the back porch, she darted away from the big house, sprinting around the goat pen, past the rhinos, her race more of a limping run as she attempted to increase speed without collapsing on her bum knee.

By the time she reached the giraffe enclosure she was out of breath and pain laced through her leg, but she still had work to do. Evangeline sucked in a deep breath and entered the barn, wasting no time slipping into Ruke's stall after opening the door.

"Okay, Ruke, you gotta move," she said, her voice equal parts tough and gentle. "The inspector is here to check on us and you have to be outside, eating grass and walking around the yard and showing all the ladies who's boss like a giraffe is supposed to do. So, get. Get!" she said again, louder, when Ruke didn't move.

Heart pounding, Evangeline timidly approached Ruke. She didn't think he'd hurt her, but being in a stall with an enormous animal was still intimidating. So she kept her movements slow, calm, one slightly shaking hand reaching out until her palm connected with coarse fur. The top of her head didn't even come up to his waist, but having touched him, feeling his heartbeat beneath her hand, she wasn't frightened. Ruke truly was a gentle giant, if only with her.

She traced her palm along his side, stroking his fur tenderly, lovingly, imagining herself speaking but sending those words through her hand, through her eyes. Her breath she kept even, matching his, though her heart beat wildly in anticipation. The giraffe flicked his tail, sending black hair into her face, and Evangeline smiled. She stepped back, fingers grazing his side.

"That's it," she whispered when she felt him move beneath her hand. "It's just outside. It's fun outside, with the other giraffes. That's it, one step at a time."

Slowly, painfully slowly, she led Ruke outside, one hand held out calmly as though bracing him, the other waving him forward. Inch by inch she stepped backward, encouraging him, guiding him, moving painstakingly slow until, finally, they both entered the sunlight.

"Good boy," she said softly, still leading him out, farther into the enclosure. She wanted to glance around frantically for signs of Jett or Mr. Tindle, but refused to break eye contact with Ruke for fear of disrupting their progress. She heard voices coming around the corner, close, too close to dart back to the barn and close the door behind her. So, she did the only thing she could do.

She hid.

Evangeline slipped behind a large rock, pressing her back against the stone just as the two men rounded the curve and came upon the entrance to the giraffe enclosure. Her heart pounded against her chest, eyes trained on Ruke, who had approached her rock and was staring back at her with his head cocked curiously.

Stay, she silently commanded him. *Don't give me away. Go ... play, or something.*

She breathed a breath of relief when Ruke took a step back and stretched upward, yanking a few leaves off the tree to his left.

"As you can see," she heard Jett say, alarmingly close, "Ruke is enjoying his time outside. And he's enjoying his afternoon snack from one of his favorite trees." There was a pause and mumbling by another voice, and then, "Well, clearly you were informed incorrectly, as I said earlier."

Evangeline listened carefully for the sounds of voices and footsteps, creeping her way along the rock to stay out of view when she heard them moving around the outside of the enclosure. Carefully, her heart still racing, she remained out of sight, one eye on the giraffes milling around and the other on the perimeter.

When she heard the two men retreating after another few minutes of discussion, Evangeline allowed herself to breathe.

LESS THAN AN hour later, Evangeline sat on the ground at the edge of the goat pen, working on her painting. She didn't have much to go, and was eager to unveil the finished piece. Half the wall was covered with a cloth, as she only uncovered the part she was working on so no prying eyes could spy. She was a strange artist in that way, afraid of judgment before a piece was finished, as though the unfinished parts would give others cause to mock her.

She paused when she sensed someone behind her, then turned to see Jett standing a couple feet away. The brush poised awkwardly in her hand, she stared up at him, waiting for him to speak.

"Looks good," he said, his voice strangely serious. "Spend the rest of the day working on it, if ya want. No chores."

"Are … Are you sure?" she asked. "I can help the keepers."

"No, take the day to do what ya want." He turned on his heel, then hesitated. "And try to stay on this side of the fence." With a wink, he walked off and disappeared into the big house.

Evangeline stared after him, lips slightly parted in surprise. Then they turned up into a smile, one that lasted her the rest of the day.

A CHANGE

JETT LEANED AGAINST the railing, dark eyes watching the activity in the giraffe enclosure. Or as close to activity as it could be considered. The animals, the gentle beasts as they were, were slow moving, leisurely enjoying their day, basking in the warmth the springtime sun had to offer.

His eyes especially watched the solitary figure standing in the back of the enclosure tugging branches off the tree. Ruke was separated from the females but watching them with interest. Jett hadn't seen that look in a while, thought the poor beast had lost it after his favored female was sent to a new home.

"He's getting better," Caster said as he approached, taking his spot next to Jett and looking out at Ruke. "Came out all on his own the past six days. Course, Evangeline

189

was standing on the outside of the fence watching him. Maybe he was just trying to get to her."

"He does seem to favor her," Jett agreed, thinking over the past week. Ever since Mr. Tindle's visit and Evangeline's renegade trip inside the enclosure, the giraffe had perked up and lost some of his surly attitude. "The vet seemed especially pleased."

"Well, yeah. With Lady Regal and all, I would be too." At Jett's blank stare, Caster laughed. "He didn't tell you this morning?"

"Dr. Bane spoke with Lettie before he left because I was on a business call. I haven't had a chance to catch up."

Caster nodded. "Well, he suspects Lady is pregnant. He's going to confirm with us soon. And since Ruke is the only male she's been out with …"

Jett laughed, thrilled by the news. His hearty voice echoed across the pasture, causing the giraffes' ears to perk up. "Well, that is fantastic news indeed! She really is helping him." His smile faded at that. "Now if we could just get him to help her back."

Caster sent his uncle a sidelong glance. "You don't think she's getting better?"

"Do you?"

He didn't answer, instead blowing out a breath. He supposed Jett was right. The teenager had her moments, minutes, hours, and even days when he thought she might be getting better. But then something would happen — a dream, a phone call — and she retreated back into that dark place in her mind where all her secrets were buried.

"Well … maybe we could invite that friend of hers who calls every now and then. I mean, she's been here a few months and only one person ever calls."

Jett eyed his nephew. "Ya know that friend is a boy, right?"

"So?"

If he was surprised by the indifferent response, he didn't show it. "I'm just saying, the friend isn't a girl. Don't want you getting all huffy if and when a new guy comes strutting in to save the damsel in distress."

Caster laughed and shook his head, his dark hair falling across his eyes and hiding any expression Jett may have been trying to read. "Jett, the girl is seventeen. She's too young for me. Don't be a creep."

Jett didn't find the age difference to be enough to warrant such a dismissal, but he brushed it aside for now. "Well then, I suppose I have a phone call to make. I'll make it happen next week, promise."

After Caster had walked away, still shaking his head over his uncle's claim, Jett turned his attention back to Ruke. The giraffe had approached cautiously. "And you," he said quietly, "it's your turn. That girl has been here for you. Now it's time you be there for her.

A WEEK LATER, Jett made true on his promise.

Evangeline stood outside the giraffe enclosure, at the place where the ground rose up and the fence dipped. She'd been spending more time here lately, rather than her place just outside the goat pen. It still hurt to sit by that fence, looking in at the goats and not seeing the one who was especially partial to her. At times she felt bad for cutting back her time there, but the others didn't seem to notice. And besides, Ruke needed her more.

She was proud of his progress since she'd arrived at Kindred Hides Wildlife Preserve. Sure, she didn't know exactly what he'd been like before he lost his female friend, but she liked to imagine he was getting back to his former self, and that she played a part in the transformation, no matter how large or small.

It was a special kind of feeling, this bond created at a place she'd been blessed with. It was a hard pill to swallow that such a blessing had come after so much tragedy. Still she heard the shattering of glass, saw the blood, so much blood, and had to accept the fact that it all led up to this moment in which she stood across the country from home, perfectly content.

She smiled when Ruke approached, eager for the treat in her hands. "Yeah, yeah, take it all," she laughed when he leaned over the railing and yanked the acacia leaves from her hands. "Easy there, piggy." The giraffe took a second bite, his long purple tongue wrapping around her wrist. "Gross."

"Just a giraffe kiss," Jett said from behind, watching and marveling over the fact that Ruke let her hand feed him. "The best kinda kiss."

Evangeline held out her hand, which dripped saliva. "If you say so," she laughed again. Her expression turned serious when Ruke paused and leaned over, his large head hovering strangely close to her own. "Hey there," she said quietly, somewhat surprised. He rarely came this close on his own, when he could clearly see that she held no more treats in either hand.

Tentatively, Evangeline reached out and rubbed a palm down the ridge on his forehead. She felt strong bone and coarse fur against her skin, warm breath on her arm. When Ruke moved forward just a step, she followed until her own forehead was resting against his own.

"Hey, boy," she greeted, a sense of oneness filling her. Her eyes closed and she breathed in the musky scent that belonged only to a giraffe, only to Ruke. In that single moment she was at peace, her hands on either side of his face, their breaths in unison. Here, she could pretend nothing else existed but Ruke and the sounds of nature.

The sounds of tranquility.

The sounds of life.

An escape from death and despair.

As though sensing her sudden turn in thoughts, Ruke pulled away, breaking the connection. Evangeline watched him return to the other giraffes with a small smile, still filled with that sense of home.

"He's yours," Jett said, voice tinged with wonder. "Ruke belongs to you, and you belong to him."

Evangeline cast him a glance over her shoulder. "What does that mean?"

"Just that. You belong to one another." When the girl didn't answer, Jett continued. "You've done a lot for him, Evangeline. He owes you. *We* owe you. And on that note …"

Evangeline followed his glance somewhere behind her, searching for whatever it was he saw.

Not whatever, she realized. *Whomever*.

A grin broke out when she saw the figure walking her way, being led down the path by Caster. Excitement, a feeling she hadn't experienced in so long she'd nearly forgotten its name, burst through her bones, fueling her for-ward.

She met Cam halfway down the path, wrapping him in a hug. His arms, those familiar arms so used to hard work on the family farm, slid around her back. For a mo-ment she could only hug him, remembering all the good times they'd shared over the years, trying hard not to think of the bad.

"What are you doing here?" she asked when she fi-nally pulled away, laughing at the grimace that formed on his face when she left behind sticky Ruke saliva on his arm. "Sorry. What are you doing here?"

"I was invited," Cam answered in his southern-twanged voice. "We wanted to surprise ya."

"I am surprised." Evangeline turned her gaze to Cast-er. "You knew?"

"It was my idea."

She considered that for a moment before taking Cam by the hand. "Come on, I want to show you everything."

As the two disappeared back toward the main house, Jett approached his nephew's side. He hid a grin at the de-jected expression Caster was trying hard not to show. "Still too young for ya?"

"Shut up."

THE REUNION

THEY SAUNTERED AROUND the preserve, Evangeline chatting about her work and Cam letting her talk. He offered a comment here and there, pointed out animals he found interesting, but most of all, rejoiced internally at the smile on her face each time they came upon a new enclosure.

She loved it here, across the country from home, in a new place with new people. That fact could have saddened him, but after her father's death and mother's transformation into a complete stranger, Evangeline was forced to find that new place and Cam couldn't fault her for finding some semblance of peace there. He could tell she still had a ways to go, considering she froze up whenever he dared to mention anything relating to her former life.

They'd always loved each other like siblings, though everyone else always thought it to be more. And because she was his sister by bond if not by blood, he had to help her heal the rest of the way.

"So this is the goat pen," Evangeline said before he could voice his thoughts. "I got started here, taking care of them. I love these little guys."

Cam joined her at the fence, gazing in at the furry bodies. "Which one is your favorite?" he asked, deciding to abandon "the talk" for now.

Her face fell a bit before she responded. "PJ … but he died a little while ago. He had a seizure or something. He … He was pretty cool though. He once butted me off that rock," she pointed, "when I was goofing off with Caster. Oh, speaking of Caster."

She took Cam by the hand and dragged him behind the enclosure, over to a wall covered with a thin cloth. "He and Jett gave me permission to paint a mural. Check it out."

She lifted the cover, Cam helping her. Once he had sight of the wall, he took a moment to stare. He'd seen dozens of Evangeline's painting before and always thought they were great, though he certainly wouldn't say he knew anything about art. But there was something different about this one, something more personal. He could see it in the perfect way the goats were painted, sunlight high-lighting their fur, round eyes of the one in the center star-ing directly at the viewer. Off to the side, a child pointed at the animals, a large smile spread across her youthful face. The girl gripped a man's hand; her father, Cam assumed. The man was also smiling, and Cam didn't miss the simi-larities between Evangeline and her dad.

In fact, he thought, the longer he observed the mural, if he had to guess, he would say she had painted herself as a child. The girl certainly looked like her, with wild auburn hair and hazel eyes, and the father matched his daughter in appearance.

But this wasn't a painting about father and daughter. Cam could tell this was solely about the goats, giving them a flower-filled pasture for play and a sunny day to bask in. The colors were vibrant, emeralds and sapphires and golden brushstrokes so evenly coated that he couldn't tell where wall began and paint ended.

"It's … pretty awesome," he complimented, breathing out a laugh. "I mean, I knew you were good, but this is … I don't know the art word for it, but it's great."

"Thanks."

He cast her a sidelong glance to see her gazing at the painting almost wistfully. "So, you're painting again, huh? That's good, Evie."

Evangeline lifted a shoulder, trying hard to dismiss the softness of his voice. "As much as I can. It still hurts my hand to hold the brush, but Caster's been helping some."

"How?"

"He massages it."

Cam hid a smile, lifting a brow instead. "Massages it, huh? What else does he *massage*?"

"Gross, Cam," Evangeline laughed and shoved his shoulder, dropping the cloth. "It's totally innocent."

"Sure it is."

"It is! He just shows me around and stuff. I'm too young for him anyway."

"Uh-huh." He let the matter drop, though not his grin

as they moved away from the wall.

They continued their walk toward the big cabin, shoving each other along the way. When they reached the bunkhouse, Evangeline's laughter floated in through the open window to the house, reaching the kitchen, where stood Jett and Lettie.

Lettie, at the stove, glanced over her shoulder at Jett, who had just taken a seat at the table to review the day's mail. "Seems you and Caster were right," she commented, stirring the gravy and thinking how nice it was to hear the girl's laughter. "That friend of hers was a good idea."

"Am I ever wrong?" Jett said back with a wry grin. He ducked to avoid the towel she threw at his head.

"No, but you must be going soft." When Jett only frowned at her, Lettie chuckled and continued stirring, wondering what he would do at her next words as she shook back her explosion of curls. "They were headed for her room. Two teenagers who haven't seen each other in months, like to wrestle around with one another, disappearing into a bedroom. Alone," she added when Jett continued to stare. She laughed again when her husband leapt up from the chair and hurried from the kitchen, all but barreling out the back door to Evangeline's room.

He didn't bother knocking, already annoyed by the closed door. Jett stomped in the bunkroom with his lips pressed together in a thin line, eyeing the two teenagers who stared back at him, confused. The girl sat in the chair at the tiny desk, booted feet propped up on the wood. The boy lay stretched out on the bed, arms behind his head ever so casually.

Before either of them could speak, Jett pointed at Cam. "You, off the bed. Never on the bed. You," he pointed to Evangeline, whose eyes were narrowed in confusion, "no boys on the bed. Ever."

With one final glare, he turned on his heel and headed for the door, pushing it open as far as it would go and propping it with a rock. He glanced back pointedly, then retreated for the big house.

When the sound of their snorts and chuckles followed him, he only retreated faster.

THE CATALYST

"SO THIS JETT guy is protective, huh?" Cam asked the next morning after breakfast, having received several more warning glances from the man. He and Evangeline were heading for the giraffes now, and he was looking forward to interacting with the animal that she credited with her healing.

"I guess so," Evangeline answered, thinking back to last night. His intrusion into her room had been unexpected, and ultimately amusing, though it did give her cause to consider. He'd been worried about … what, she wondered. Her virtue? The thought made her laugh, but also appreciate the fact that he cared.

Like a father, she thought.

"He called me his little elf once," she said distractedly. "Just like Dad used to. It was … weird, but in a good way, I guess."

Cam chewed on the inside of his cheek, mulling over her words. He saw the way she and Jett interacted, and he was beginning to suspect he was taking on the role of *father*. He wasn't sure if that was good for Evangeline or something that would cause more heartache when her time at the preserve was over, but he couldn't fault either of them for bonding. "Well, you can tell him he doesn't have to worry about us being alone in your room. I'm not particularly fond of making out with my sister."

Evangeline huffed. "Like I'd want to hook up with a guy who's like my brother? Please."

"Especially when ya got eyes for the boss's nephew."

"I do not! You're so irritating." Evangeline punched his shoulder while Cam only laughed. "Anyway, that's Ruke, out there by the rocks. The one sitting next to him is Lady Regal. They call her Lady. They also said she's pregnant."

Cam looked out at the two giraffes, seeming so peaceful in the sun. "Way to go, Ruke," he said teasingly. "So this is the guy you love so much?"

"He is," Evangeline agreed. "He's gorgeous. And smart. And definitely has his own stubborn personality."

"Stubborn, huh? No wonder you two get along."

"Bite me," Evangeline retorted, though she had to admit he was partially right. She liked Ruke's stubbornness, found it charming and relatable. "Anyway, I know it kind of sounds weird, but he's helped me a lot. It feels like he understands when I talk to him about all the bad stuff that's happened this past year."

Cam hesitated, his hands gripping the fence, then

asked, "About that … When are ya gonna tell me what happened?"

She didn't look at him. "You know what happened."

"I know what happened with your dad and the accident. Not … the other." He gestured to her wrist, which was still covered with the thick bracelet.

"Oh." Evangeline dropped her arm to her side, wanting to hide what he had already seen. "It's not important."

"You know that's not true."

"It's for me to worry about."

"Like with your dad?" Cam crossed his arms when she turned her steely hazel eyes to him. "Don't look at me like that, Evie. I told ya that I was gonna say something if you didn't. I mean it. So, ya need to do something."

"What good would it do?" she shot back, anger building until her stomach and chest burned. "It's done. He's *dead*, Cam. It wouldn't change *anything*!"

"It would change what your mom thinks of you."

"At the expense of my father!" she shouted, not able to keep herself from yelling. "I won't do that to him, or to her! No matter what she's done!"

"What has she done, Evie? What did she do to you, or say, that made you do *this*." He grabbed her wrist, holding it tightly when she tried to pull away. "Tell me the truth, Evie, because if ya don't, I'm gonna tell your mom the truth of that day."

Evangeline yanked her wrist out of his grasp, a sob stuck in her throat, pushed back by bitter anger. "Don't you threaten me, Cam. Don't you dare try to give me an ultimatum like that. You don't understand what you're asking me to do. And for what? So you'll feel better?"

"No, you idiot, so *you'll* feel better!" Cam shouted

back, eyes bright with anger. "You really think this is all about me? Come on, Evie, you know me better than that! I want *you* to get better and come home, and the only way you can do that is by facing the truth!"

They squared off against one another for a tense, silent moment, jaws clenched, eyes narrowed. All the words they'd said over the years — and all the ones they hadn't — hovered between them, threatening to end whatever relationship they'd built as friends lest they mend the frayed bond between them.

Finally Evangeline broke and took a step back. "I'm done with this," she snapped, then spun around and stalked away before he could respond, knowing he wouldn't follow. Cam didn't like confrontation, especially with girls.

When she rounded the corner, Evangeline nearly ran face first into Caster, who was leaning against the barn wall with his arms crossed. He gave her an interested yet sad stare that she returned through watery eyes, before he, too, was left behind.

CASTER ENTERED THE big house, ready for a hearty meal after a long day pulling double duty. With Ash gone and Evangeline preoccupied with Cam, the extra workload was left to him to handle. Usually he didn't mind, but today he was feeling the extra weight.

When he entered the kitchen, he found Jett wearing a groove in the floor while Lettie and Cam bickered at one another. The rest of the preserve staff sat at the table, watching the drama unfold, not daring to ask when dinner would be served.

"What's going on?" he addressed the group, a bit unnerved when all eyes turned to him.

"Have you seen Evie?" Cam replied, his face a portrait of both concern and annoyance.

"Not since ... earlier, at the giraffe barn," Caster said, knowing the teenager would catch on to his meaning. "I figured she just went for a walk. She's not back?"

"No, and we've looked everywhere," Jett put in, running a worried hand through his thick black hair. "It's almost dark. She disappeared after she and Cam had a fight. Seems Cam here didn't think it necessary to go after her, even considering her past."

"I knew she wanted to be alone, but I didn't think she'd go into hiding," Cam muttered. Caster got the feeling he was battling between concern and flat-out annoyance. He nearly grinned, considering the girl made him feel the same way at times.

Then Cam's words sunk in. Wanting to be alone, a place to hide. There was only one place at the preserve where anyone could get away.

"I think I might know where she is. But I'm going alone," Caster added when Cam and Jett both perked up. "She's pissed enough at you, Cam, and I doubt she wants to see an adult, Jett."

"*You* are an adult, Caster."

"Fine, an *old* adult," Caster answered Jett with a smirk. "I'll go get her. You guys just sit and eat."

The others agreed, though with some amount of grumbling, so Caster first grabbed a piece of chicken off the stove and held it between his teeth, then jogged to the storage room for a flashlight and lantern — top-of-the-line gear he would need for a trek through the woods — before heading out. He cursed to himself while gathering the items, not at all pleased by the idea of walking through spiderwebs and thorny branches in the dark, and fully intending to give Evangeline a piece of his mind when he found her.

It took him nearly an hour to make his way to the waterfall, nearly sixty minutes of tripping over bush and branch while attempting to scarf down his meager meal until, finally, he pushed his way through to the clearing. He stood in place for a moment, shining the light around, a feeling of dread building when he didn't see her.

"Caster?"

A quiet voice to his right had Caster reeling around, shining the light in the direction of the sound. When he saw Evangeline flinch as the brightness hit her eyes, he sighed. "Christ, girl, you scared the hell out of me. Out of all of us."

To his surprise, Evangeline rushed forward and grabbed him in a hug. He held an arm around her, feeling her trembling against him. "I scared myself," she admitted, pulling back. "I came out here to think and before I knew it, it was dark and there was no way I could find my way back home."

Home.

The word interested him, but he would have to mull over it later. "What the hell happened? I mean ... I know you know I heard you fighting, but I don't know the details."

"We just, had a fight," she answered off-handedly.

"Don't give me that," Caster shot back. "I walked through the woods in pitch-black night to come get you, so you owe me a little more than 'we had a fight.'"

"I don't owe you anything. Or Cam."

"Well, I have a feeling *that's* not true," Caster said wryly, noting the irritation in her face, which was shadowed by the flashlight. Good. The more he annoyed her, the more likely she was to tell him what he wanted to know. "Why are you so afraid of telling the truth?"

When she didn't answer, instead appearing to have some sort of internal battle with herself, Caster softened and lowered himself to a rock along the water's edge, gesturing for her to join him. He had a feeling she sat next to him because he had the light rather than actually relenting.

"Evangeline … do you know the history of the preserve's Second Hides Program?"

The question surprised her, not having been expected. When she thought about it, she realized she actually knew next to nothing about the program Rick claimed would help her get her life back on track. "Just that it was started to help troubled teens, give them guidance, get them back on track. Rick said they only take one teen at a time to make sure he or she gets their sole attention."

"Right, but do you know how it started? Or why it was started, rather?"

Evangeline shrugged. "I never really cared enough to ask, I guess. It didn't seem to matter. Why?" she pressed after a moment of silence. "Why was it started?"

Caster let out a breath, wondering how she would react to what he said next. "It was started for me."

REVELATIONS

EVANGELINE STARED THROUGH the night at the figure next to her. The lantern cast his face in a mix of orange and shadow, hiding all the things he'd never told her about his past. In that moment, she realized she didn't know much about Caster except his love for animals and the preserve, along with his tendency to nose in on conversations that had nothing to do with him. It had never occurred to her to ask about his life, his childhood, too blinded by her own selfish grief to attempt to care about anyone else.

Selfish.

Her mother called her that once. She wouldn't be what her mother believed.

Evangeline cleared her throat and pushed the topic. It

felt awkward, prying into someone else's life, but also felt welcomed. "What do you mean?"

Caster sat up a little straighter, not liking what he was going to reveal but knowing she needed to hear it nonetheless. "I mean, I was the original troubled teen. For this program, anyway." He thought back to just over ten years ago. "My parents divorced when I was eleven, and let's just say I didn't take it very well, especially when my dad remarried about three months later. He pretty much forgot about me, had another kid with another woman, and that was that." It still hurt, his father all but abandoning him, sending a birthday card once a year and maybe a Christmas present if he remembered. Even now they rarely spoke, and saw each other only by chance.

"I started doing the stereotypical angry teen crap. Getting into fights, not listening to anyone, not doing homework. That went on for about a year or so. A little after I turned thirteen, I found myself in with the bad crowd. A group of older guys and a few girls. Our school combined middle and high, so it wasn't hard to find the troublemakers of all ages."

He paused, remembering his sorry punk behavior back then. It was embarrassing, knowing the kid he used to be. "I put my mom through hell and back until finally I was stupid enough to join the crowd when they decided to break into a convenience store for beer." Caster laughed a sarcastic laugh. "Like I said, such a stereotype. Anyway, we got caught and let's just say the options weren't looking good for me. Kind of a, three strikes and you're out thing. That was when Jett stepped in. Apparently he'd been looking for a way to give back to the community through his preserve, and when my mom told him about everything, he thought up the program. He got everything set up before I even knew what was happening, and I was shipped off to the preserve without even getting a say in the matter."

Evangeline tried to imagine a young trouble-making Caster, but found it a difficult image to visualize. Mischievous, sure, but not criminal. "But … you're so *not* like that now."

Caster chuckled. "Well, I guess you could say the program worked. Jett brought me out here and whipped me into shape. You know how he is. He makes you feel like you belong, like you're doing something great. That's the whole point of the program, where its name comes from. Second Hides. Like you're shedding your old skin and growing into someone new, someone better. Your second skin, second life. Second chance. You get the picture."

Evangeline nodded, and Caster continued. "When my time was up here, I didn't want to go home. This place *was* home. I made it about another year with my mom before I convinced her to let me come back and homeschool. So I did that, graduated on my own, and never really looked back, especially when Jett started talking about expanding the preserve to do conservation work in Africa. There have been other kids come through the program, some staying longer than others, some keeping on the good road afterwards and some not. Just depends on the kid, I guess, and how invested they get in this place."

He stole a glance over at Evangeline, saw her wrestling again with her thoughts, needing more time to gather the courage to speak. "So, long story short, I know it sucks to get sent out here at first, kind of feels like everyone gave up on you and just wanted you gone. But the program works, if you let it. I'm proof of that, since I'm such an outstanding guy and all." He shot her a mischievous grin that had her laughing. "I go back to my mom's a few times a year to say hi, hang out, try to make up for all the crap I put her through. But this will always be home."

Evangeline swallowed hard, swallowed back her tears as she whispered, "I don't have a home."

When she fell silent, Caster turned to face her a little more and asked, "Will you tell me about it?" His voice was just as quiet as hers, only the echo of crickets and frogs surrounding them.

"I … I don't know where to start."

"Start from that day," he suggested softly. "The day you lost him."

A tear slid down her cheek as she tried hard, so hard, to keep in the truth. But the pain of holding in her words was too much to bear, and so, finally, she revealed what happened that day.

Sunlight streamed in through the curtains, but the teenage girl still rested snugly in bed. It wasn't until a knocking on her door sounded that she stirred.

"Come on, little elf. Time for your lesson." A head popped into her room, followed by a body. Her father stood in the doorway with a wide grin spreading across his face. Keys jingled in one of his hands, much to the girl's annoyance.

"Dad. It's Sunday, the day of rest," Evangeline mumbled from beneath the covers.

The man laughed, the corners of his blue eyes crinkling as he leaned over and shook his daughter's mattress.

"The Frosts never rest! We're always up for adventure! Get ready, we're going driving!"

Begrudgingly, the sixteen-year-old dragged herself out of bed and got ready for the day. It was only a half hour later that she joined her father in their Jeep — this time with her in the driver's seat.

"Hey now, none of that sourpuss face," her father playfully chastised when he glanced over to see her scowling. "It's not that *early. Besides, your birthday is coming up, which means your drivers license test!"*

"Yeah, yeah," Evangeline grumbled as she started the engine. Her scowl turned to a grin when the radio began blaring the sounds of Queen's Bohemian Rhapsody. *"Seriously?"*

"Gotta get pumped up for the road!"

"You are such an old man."

But she turned the song up anyway and they pulled out of the driveway, her father head-banging in the seat next to her. He had always loved music, and, though they may not share the same tastes, she had to admit his enthusiasm was infectious.

That excitement carried them through the neighborhood, where she kept to the slow speed limit and carefully made her way around turns. "It's a nice day," she commented, mostly for the sake of conversation. "I love the color of the sky and how green the grass is. It'd make a great painting."

Her father looked out the window as though visualizing the landscape as art. "Paint me a picture, little elf."

"Maybe, if you're good," she teased, and her father stuck his tongue out at her. It wasn't until they pulled into the main street that she began to feel nervous, only having

driven a few times before on busy roads.

"What's next?" she asked, eyes trained on the road before them.

"Changing lanes, little elf," her father answered. "The road is yours to command! The High Queen of Florida!"

She laughed at that, rolling her eyes at his display of grandeur. Always outgoing, never dull, her father could make even the grumpiest of men and women roll with laughter. But she admired that about him, his openness and friendliness, as well as his ability to recognize the seriousness of any situation.

"Don't forget your blinker. Check your blind spots. Good. See, piece of cake."

"Yeah, you owe me some."

"You don't even like cake."

"No, but I like presents."

He laughed, a rich sound that filled the car. "Yeah, yeah. Keep your eyes on the road, princess."

She did just that, watching out for dangers, keeping a close eye on the other drivers. Evangeline considered herself a good driver, the few times she had been out, but she wanted to feel like she was completely ready for her test. Failing wasn't an option, not on her birthday. Not any time, really.

Eventually they made their way to the highway. Being that it was Sunday, the lanes were relatively clear, but enough cars and semis passed by to make her hesitant.

"Easy now," he said, his voice gentle to quell her rising nerves. "Turn gently, let the wheel slide through your hands."

She followed his voice, each movement matching his

softly spoken words. A successful maneuver, one that awarded her a smile and pat on the shoulder.

"Nice work, my little elf," he said, his nickname reaching her ears with affection. "Just go with the flow," he directed, settling back in the seat. "One car length behind the one in front."

The road took them on a silent journey, each concentrating on thoughts not spoken. Her — delight in overcoming fear, joy in the feel of such freedom. Him — compassion for the young girl's nerves, pride in her courage.

Her cell phone rang, vibrating in the center console cupholder and bringing them both out of their reverie. Evangeline glanced down at it, wondering who would bother calling her on a Sunday morning, before turning back to the road.

"Expecting a call?" her dad teased, then picked up the phone and looked at the screen. "Ah, it's Mr. Cam, calling on my daughter."

"Dad," Evangeline admonished while rolling her eyes. Those eyes widened when she saw that he had answered the call. "What are you doing!"

"Hello, Evie's father speaking, why have you called upon my daughter?" he spoke into the phone, ignoring her protests. He was quiet for a moment, Evangeline torn between needing to watch the road and wanting to know what was being said. "Well now, that's interesting."

"What? What does Cam want?"

"Oh, just to chat about the prom. After all, your senior year is coming up. Methinks someone has a crush. What's that?" He turned back to the cell phone conversation. "You're just friends? I've heard that before. You'd be lucky to have my little elf on your arm." His tone was seri-

ous, but the grin on his face told Evangeline that Cam was along for the ride.

Suddenly he held the phone out toward Evangeline. "Someone wants to ask you a question."

"Please, Dad." She rolled her eyes, sparing him a moment's glance. "It's not like that."

"Nope. Father knows best."

"Don't think so."

"I think it's sweet. My little elf and the boy whose legs I'll have to break if he breaks your heart."

"Dad! He can hear you!" She huffed, annoyance clear in her tone. "Since when do you care about my love life anyway?"

"I'm your dad. I always care."

"How convenient."

Her father huffed too, mimicking her earlier action. Then he held out the phone. "Cammy boy wants to talk to you."

"Tell him I'll call him back."

He held the phone to his ear. "She said to tell you she'd love to be your date. And that she expects a kiss at the end of the night. A PG kiss, mind you. None of that gross tongue action."

"Dad! Come on!" Her temper started to flare at that. God only knew what Cam would think of this little exchange. They'd been best friends since they were kids and never even once shared a kiss out of curiosity. They were like siblings, despite what everyone else thought.

"My little elf has a boyfriend."

"Dad!"

"Evie girl and the boy down the street."

Her grip tightened on the wheel. "Dad, no way!"

"I heard it all myself. There's no hiding true love from me!" Her father laughed his hearty laugh, then pressed the phone to her ear. *"Better grab him up while you can."*

She shrugged off the phone. *"Dad, quit it! Come on. You're distracting me."*

"Excuses, excuses," he chuckled, picking up his traveler's mug of coffee and taking a sip. *"I think we've embarrassed our Evie girl,"* he said into the phone, pausing while Cam replied too softly for Evangeline to hear. *"Oh really? Well now maybe that will make her stop looking at me like I haven't bathed in a month. Here."* He held the phone up to her again, only to have Evangeline swat at him.

She hit his hand harder than she intended and the phone flew from his grip, smacking her father in the side of the face. Out of instinct he flinched and jerked, coffee spilling out of his mug and all over Evangeline's lap. The burning-hot liquid seared against her bare knees and thighs.

"Ow! Dad, it's burning me!" she yelled, desperately wiping at her legs with one hand while her other gripped the wheel.

"Calm down!" he shouted back, taking the wheel when she cried out in pain. But it was too late. The Jeep swerved into the middle lane, clipping the small car speeding up the side. The Jeep spun, tipping dangerously on its side. The semi coming up from behind tipped it the rest of the way.

A crash of metal, crunching of doors, the world turned upside down.

Confusion amidst pain. The sky turning to road.

Laughter turning into screams.

Skin stained red.

She didn't know how many times the Jeep flipped, how long it took to come to a stop, only that finally, at some point, she opened her eyes.

Confusion consumed her, her eyes not able to comprehend why the sky was ground and the earth not where it should be and everything around her broken and smashed. Her vision was fuzzy, streaked with red tears, as she searched her surroundings, a buzzing in her ears drowning out the sounds of the road. Shattered glass littered the scene, pieces of metal crunched against her, trapping her knee.

Only then did she feel the pain. Deep, agonizing pain everywhere in her body, radiating out from throbbing pinpoints she tried desperately not to think about. Her right knee, her leg that refused to move no matter how many times she commanded it to. Her face, something cold and sharp sticking out of it. Her hand, mangled, she realized when she lifted it to touch her jaw.

An accident. She'd been in a car accident. But how? A phone call, her thoughts reminded her. Cam. Prom. Her dad teasing her.

Dad.

"Daddy?" she whispered, looking through streaks of red at the figure next to her, hanging precariously upside down. Blood, so much blood, an unnatural amount coming from him, from wounds that she feared could never be mended. Sounds, noises that would haunt her forever, escaping his lips.

"I ... sorry, little elf." The words were pained, gurgled through a throat sliced with metal. Evangeline

reached out, touched his face, his cold, shuddering face. "I ... love you. And ... your mom. Tell her ... for me ..."

"No." Her voice was weak, but the single word forced open her father's eyes. They were watery, distant, unfocused. "You tell her. Stay with me and tell her yourself." Evangeline watched her father, seeing his labored breaths, smelling the blood, so much blood.

Horns blasting, tires squealing.

Evangeline turned her eyes to the shattered windshield, seeing road as sky and sky as blood, so much blood. She glanced over at her father, her eyes seeing what his couldn't — the approaching shadow of dark metal that couldn't stop in time. Panic and pain turned to urgency.

Her father saw the change, knew what it meant.

"Daddy," she choked out, unable to say the words.

He said them for her. "Stay strong, little elf. Stay strong for me."

And then the world ended.

31

A STEP TOWARD HEALING

THE NIGHT DESCENDED upon them, cloaking the duo in heavy truths. Evangeline — struggling to whitewash memories of her father's mangled body, trying so hard to unsee the blood, so much blood. Caster — searching his mind for the right words to say to the girl who saw something that would haunt her nightmares for the rest of her life.

There were no words that could change the past or make it right. There were no promises, no condolences, no expressions of regret, to erase the pain of that day. Only time would allow Evangeline's memories to fade.

After a while, Caster let out a deep breath and risked a glance over at Evangeline. She was staring at the ground; even in the dark, he could see that her eyes were red and her hands nearly white from clutching one another. "He distracted you," he surmised, deciding to go for the obvious rather than the sympathetic. "The phone, the coffee."

"It was so stupid," Evangeline whispered, not quite able to confirm his claim. "Just ... goofing around at the wrong time. And I hit his hand, and the coffee spilled, and …"

Caster frowned. "But it wasn't your fault. Is that what you've been hiding? That he distracted you?"

She sucked in a deep breath, her heart heavy. "Phone records were pulled after the accident, since I was at fault. They knew Cam called. I guess Cam also sent a couple texts that my dad must have read without me knowing. They assumed I was on the phone and even texting. They said I was distracted. Charges were filed initially by one of the other drivers who was in the accident, but she ended up dropping them. I never found out why. Maybe because Dad was the only one who died and she felt bad. So instead of potentially facing jail I had a fine to pay and something about not being able to get my license for a while. I don't really know how long. I don't want it anyway so I didn't really pay attention."

"And you never told the truth." When Evangeline just shook her head, Cam's eyes narrowed in confusion. "Why not?"

"Because ... Because my dad was the best person I've ever known. Everyone always said he was the kind of person you should aspire to be. He was generous and smart and friendly and always made good choices. But he made a mistake that day. If I told people the truth, they would think less of him, and everything he'd ever worked for would be for nothing. I know what they would say about him … the same stuff they say about me. And my mom …" The thought of her mother hurt worst of all. "She idolized him. They were the perfect couple. Happy, in love. To tell the truth … I'd be ruining that perfect image she has of him. His death destroyed her, turned her into this … alcoholic who can't function without him in her life. Me saying he distracted me and that it was partially his fault? That *he* was on the phone and spilled coffee on his daughter, causing her to wreck? I think it would kill her."

A noble cause, Caster managed to think between her words, but an unnecessary one. Evangeline was, for all intents and purposes, just a kid. She shouldn't have to live with someone else's guilt. "Your mom. Isn't she kind of why you're here?" When Evangeline looked over at him suspiciously, he lifted a shoulder. "So I eavesdrop."

"Yeah. It's a very unflattering quality."

"So sue me," he responded to her sarcastic reply. "What did she do?"

She heaved a sad sigh. "She didn't do anything."

He stared at her face, trying to hear what she wasn't saying. Maybe not doing anything was the problem. Not taking her daughter to physical therapy. Not being able to help Evangeline through her grief. Not making her feel loved or even wanted.

No, Caster decided. It wasn't action or inaction that led to Evangeline's attempted suicide. It was something deeper.

"What did she say?"

That was the question she didn't want to answer. The question everyone had been asking for so long now. The question that had an answer, but one that broke her heart every single day.

Evangeline turned her wrist over, looking down at the leather that was tied across her skin. With trembling fingers, she untied the strips and pulled away the edges until the scar glowed against the lantern light. The wound was dark red and jagged, a permanent reminder of the night she wished her life lost.

Caster's eyes locked on the scar and he swallowed hard. He'd been expecting something smaller, a thin white line like all the healed cuts he had on his arms and shoulders after years of physical labor at the preserve. But this, this was beyond expectation, an ugly and shockingly long reminder of something so painful that only death allowed escape.

He took her wrist gently. "What did she say, Evie?"

Words stuck in her throat. Words, so simple, so impossible to say aloud. She didn't have the strength to hear them again. She didn't have the strength not to.

"I wish it had been you, not him."

If he was angry, or shocked, or amused, or felt any emotion at all to such cruel words, he didn't show it. Instead, Caster lifted her wrist and placed a soft kiss on the scar. It wasn't a romantic kiss, Evangeline noted with some amount of relief, but one of comfort, a gesture that reminded her she wasn't alone.

"You need to tell this to Rick," he said. "You need to talk to someone who has the capability to … you know … help you."

Her shoulders slumped at that and she withdrew her arm from his grasp. "I don't want to say it all again," she sighed. "One time was enough."

"Then I'll tell him. And I'll tell him that it's only between you two, not anyone else."

Evangeline thought about it for a moment before finally nodding. After another hesitation, she added, "You want to know the really stupid thing about it? Cam didn't even call about prom. He called to tell me about the new dirt bike he got. We were supposed to go riding that weekend."

A snort escaped before he could stop it. Caster held up his hands when Evangeline shot him a dirty look. "Sorry. I just don't picture you as the type of girl to go dirt biking."

"Yeah, well ... I was different back then. Better."

"I think you're just fine now. Temper tantrums and all." He gave her a playful grin, one that disappeared quickly when he thought of something else. "What made you change your mind?"

"What?"

He gestured to her wrist, which she had covered again with the bracelet. "You didn't do the other wrist."

"Oh." Evangeline heaved a breath, thinking back to that night. "Something my dad said to me the day of the accident. Everyone ... the doctors and all ... they said he died immediately, on impact, because of his injuries. But ... he didn't." She swallowed back the tears and the bitter taste of bile that burned the back of her throat. "I never admitted the truth because I didn't want anyone, especially Mom, to know that his last few moments were so painful and scary for him. It's better for everyone to think that he was never in pain." She hated knowing what no one else did, seeing over and over again her father in his last minute of life.

"There was no way he should have lived. I don't pretend to understand it. There was so much blood ... He told me to stay strong for him. The night I did this," she lifted her arm briefly, "I was sitting there, bleeding out, and that memory came to me. And, I don't know, it reminded me that I'm supposed to live, for him, for me. So, I called for help."

Caster recalled Jett telling him about the accident. Seven people had been injured, but only one died. And the one who didn't make it was said to have died on impact, having lost so much blood from a piece of metal that sliced through an artery, among other serious wounds. For three months now he'd wondered what it must have been like for Evangeline, waking up in her state of delirium at the scene of the accident, seeing her father next to her, no longer of the living. And now he knew all his wondering had been for naught. It wasn't the memory of her deceased father that haunted her most, but of his final moments.

Even in death, though, her father was there for this daughter, giving her the guidance she needed. Caster was willing to be the one who guided her in life. "You took the first step, then. You've been resisting everything since you got here, but the fact is, you took the first step. Now, it's time to take the rest."

A FRIENDSHIP REKINDLED

THREE DAYS PASSED, time filled with uncomfortable silence and, yet, the promise of a brighter tomorrow. Evangeline allowed Caster to reveal her secrets to the ones she couldn't confess to, and was grateful when they didn't press her for details. Jett and Lettie kept their distance, allowing her the space to heal. Caster showed her to her work with as few words as possible. Rick wrote down notes and muttered to himself about holding people accountable.

Cam, though, demanded more from her.

He walked with her to the giraffe barn, hands shoved in his pockets. They hadn't yet talked about her confession to Caster, and she sensed it was coming. For a while they worked, shoveling hay out of the barn and replenishing it, cleaning out water dishes, organizing the shelves. Finally they moved outside to stock the hay feeders along the fence. All the while Cam wondered how he got himself roped into manual labor, but he pretended that he didn't mind since it still got him out of school for a few days.

After making almost a complete circle around the enclosure, Evangeline couldn't stand the tense silence any longer. "Cam, I thought about what you said." She waited until he looked up at her, then sighed. "Just … hear me out before you argue, okay?" When he frowned at her, she took it as agreement. "I know you want to tell my mom the truth. I know why you feel the way you do."

"Do you?" he asked, the question both curious and annoyed. "I called you, Evie. I could have hung up when your dad answered. I could have said I'd call you back instead of playing along with him. I could have told him to stop goofing off and let you drive. But I didn't. I laughed with him and told him to tease you, because we thought it was funny. And look what happened."

"Cam …" She had to admit, she'd never thought of it like that before. Nor had she known that he had played along. All this time she'd thought her dad had been giving them both a hard time, embarrassing them both. But, knowing better now didn't change anything. "It's not your fault. All you did was make a phone call. You couldn't have known we were in the car. Dad goofing off wasn't your fault."

"If I hadn't of called—"

"It doesn't matter," she cut in, surprised at how bitter her tone sounded. "You did call. I keep thinking, Dad should have known better. He was the adult in the situation, so he should have stopped it before it went that far.

225

But so what? We aren't stupid. We knew it was wrong too. We could have been responsible."

She could tell Cam was trying hard not to say anything to that little confession, so she charged forward. "What's done is done, and I, for one, am so freaking tired of thinking 'what if' over and over and over again, because it doesn't matter. And you know what?" Her temper rose as she turned on him. "This isn't your secret to tell. It's mine. It's my dad, my mom, my family. *I* get to decide what my mom's final memories of my dad are. *I* get to decide what people know of our last moments together. Not you. I'm sorry for what happened. I'm sorry that you're hurting and that you feel guilty and that you can't make everything better again. But this is my life and my family and *I* get to decide what guilt to live with. So you … you just need to get over it!"

The shock of her words froze him, hands grasping a bale of alfalfa hay. Behind him, on the other side of the fence, Ruke sauntered over, his attention caught by the sound of Evangeline's raised voice. Cam didn't turn, or even acknowledge the new presence. Instead, he glared at his childhood friend, tempted to throw the hay bale at her.

Get over it? That was her solution? Fine. He could play that game.

"Well … maybe you just need to get over it too," he shot back, not sure if he truly meant it or was just trying to hurt her as much as those words hurt him.

She stared at Cam, letting the words fill her, strengthen her, rather than destroy. "Maybe you're right," she answered in a whisper. "Maybe I do." Evangeline tried to read the thoughts in his stormy eyes.

I won't do it.

You're a moron.
You can't get over it.
Whatever.

But she also sensed something else, an underlying agreement, a silent promise that, as her best friend, he would do as she asked. Knowing that made all the hurt feelings caused by their arguing go away, the anger smoothed out by a bond strong enough to survive this test of friendship.

"You gonna stand there all day or feed Ruke?" she finally asked, hoping to avoid further argument or awkward silence.

"Huh?"

Evangeline pointed behind her at Ruke, who had approached the edge of the fence and was eying the hay curiously. Cam started to turn, but, before she could warn him, the giraffe lowered his head and swept it quickly to the side, knocking Cam upside the head with his ossicones.

Cam fell to the side and dropped to his knee, on top of the hay bale. With one hand he held his head, with the other he braced himself against the ground. He lay there for a moment, gathering his wits and bearings, then scowled up at Ruke. The giraffe was peering down at him expectantly, not quite able to reach the hay now spread across the grass.

Cam's eyes turned to Evangeline when he heard a snort come from her direction. "Excuse me?"

She couldn't hold it in. Evangeline laughed, the combination of Cam's aggravated expression and Ruke's impatient grunts filling her with delight. Even when Cam threw the rest of the bale at her, striking her in the chest, still she laughed until finally he joined her, abandoning his irritation in favor of humor.

"He's a little grumpy," Evangeline giggled out. She approached the fence, expecting Ruke to back up and walk away, surprised when he stayed.

"You can say that again," Cam mumbled, though a grin still teased his cheeks. "Hey, what are you doing? Don't get so close."

"He won't hurt me. He likes me. He likes you too; you just deserved a good head-butt."

"Evie, seriously. It's a wild animal. Stay back."

His words went unheard as Evangeline stopped in front of Ruke, whose head hung low, level with hers. "Don't be a bully," she whispered to him, one hand on either side of his face. "You be nice. Cam is good people."

"Cam is awesome people," her friend put in from his place on the ground.

Evangeline shushed him, then turned back to Ruke, who she swore was frowning back at her. "Aw, come on, buddy. He's just a smelly ole' human friend. We all know you're my main guy. So be nice. Laugh with us. Feel alive again." She leaned over until her forehead touched his. They stood together, mended one another's broken hearts, one breath at a time. After a moment, she lifted her gaze to his deep chocolate eyes and kissed him right between them.

When she looked back at Cam, she saw him watching the scene, a perplexed expression crossing his tanned face. "What?"

Cam picked himself up, brushing off his jeans. "Nothing. Just never thought you'd be besties with a giraffe."

"Besties?" Evangeline repeated, one eyebrow cocked.

"Since when did you go Valley Girl on me?"

"Yeah, that was weird, wasn't it?"

They both laughed again, then cleaned up the spilled hay and headed in for lunch at the sound of Lettie's bell.

33

PREPARATION

A KNOCK SOUNDED at her door. Evangeline called the person in, grateful for the break from her schoolwork. Rick entered with a soft smile. Sunlight streamed in behind him, haloing the caseworker in a golden aura that nearly had Evangeline rolling her eyes.

He had arrived only yesterday for another random checkup, though Evangeline doubted it was as random as he claimed. Showing up only days after her confession to Caster and Cam's departure? No, Rick was here for a purpose, and she knew she had to play her part well.

"Morning," he greeted, taking a seat in the second chair. "I wanted to catch you before you got going today."

She wrote her name at the top of a worksheet and added it to the stack next to her, then handed it all to Rick.

"These are all my assignments for the week. I finished them early."

He accepted the papers, noting that she held the pencil in her right-hand fingers with ease. Jett had kept him up-to-date with both her schoolwork and her injuries, assuring him that while she was healing slowly, she was healing nonetheless. "You've been busy."

"Yeah, well, Cam went home a few days ago so I had free time again. It seemed like a lot more than usual though."

"That's because it was." At her frown, Rick explained, "I've had your tutor slipping in additional lessons and homework."

"Why?"

"So you could graduate early." Rick chuckled at the surprise in her face, though it was a laugh tinged with sadness. "I know school has been hard for you the past year and that you were worried about graduation because of how much school you've missed. I'm sure the last thing you'd want to do is repeat your senior year." He knew he figured right when he saw the look of relief in her eyes. "So, your tutor and I decided to make sure that wouldn't happen. Now you can go home knowing you will be a high school graduate and that you won't have to worry about school. As you know, I've been meeting with your mother throughout your time here, and obviously meeting with you. I know how hard it can be for teens to return home after time spent in any sort of program, and I want to make this transition easier for you. I don't want you to worry."

"… About what?"

Rick offered the girl a small smile, his eyes kind. "About slipping into bad habits or repeating past mistakes."

Evangeline sat back, not sure what to say. Had she been that transparent? Was it that obvious that her home life was in the toilet and there was nothing left for her back in Florida? Had he been that worried that she would continue down a dark path if she returned home?

If she returned home.

When she returned home.

She *would* go home. Back to a home no longer warmed by her father's laugh. Back to a shell of a place that once felt safe. Back to the figure once familiar but now long since strange.

Mother.

Evangeline cleared her throat. "Um … what do I have to do to graduate?"

Rick smiled again, attempting to comfort the teenager, having seen the effect his earlier words had on her. "A few tests, a couple meetings. I'll arrange everything. I don't want you to worry about it. Instead, it's time to prepare. I spoke with your mother yesterday and stopped by your house to make sure everything looked good. She sounded eager to have you home. Said she'd have your room ready and that she'd pick you up from the airport. So, with that settled, we look to what we have to do on this side of the country. You only have a couple more weeks here."

"Then back home?"

"Then back home."

"What then?"

Setting the stack of papers across his lap, Rick leaned back and thought about the question. What then? What did the future hold for one Evangeline Lorelei Frost? "Then, whatever you make of it. Do you want to go to college? Do you want to continue with your art? Do you have any ideas for what job you may like? Knowing what you want to do when you return will help you stay focused, make sure you don't slip down the wrong path."

"I won't," she promised. It was a vow she fully intended to keep.

TWO WEEKS LATER, Evangeline awoke to the knowledge that today she would say good-bye. Good-bye to the place that had become a second home. Good-bye to the people who had transformed her life and made her feel whole. Good-bye to the animal that gave her life meaning again.

The thought of so many good-byes made it hard to get out of bed, but eventually she did rise. Her movements were slow, forced, each one bringing her closer to that moment when she would leave everything and everyone she loved behind.

Breakfast in the big house was a lively affair, though tinged with the fact no one wanted to acknowledge. Evangeline slipped out quietly after everyone had eaten, deciding to make her rounds — and her farewells — alone.

She stopped at the elephants first, watching them wander around the enclosure, one playing with a tire that had been tossed out in the middle the previous day. The little one, Sterling, was splashing around in the shallow end of the watering hole while the other large gray beasts went about their days carelessly, with no regard to the one who would not be staying.

Next she found herself at the Eastern Bongos. Like Caster, the Bongos had always fascinated her, with their intriguing mix of reddish-gold fur and the elegant twists of horns. One of them approached the fence and allowed her to pet its nose before returning to the edge of the pond to graze.

At the goat pen she hesitated, but made her way inside to the rock PJ had once claimed for himself. She stood atop the stone, hands on her hips, mind replaying the day she had finally come out of her hollow shell of depression, even if only for a moment.

"I am the goat goddess," she whispered with a sad smile, all over again feeling PJ head-butting her knee. Her fingers grazed over the scar on her head where she'd struck it against the rock, then moved to the goat that approached her after she'd squatted down. Chadster nibbled at her empty hand, searching for treats. She scratched him behind the ears and rubbed his growing belly playfully, knowing that as hard as it had been to lose PJ, getting to spend time with these adorable little guys had been worth the heartache.

Eventually she made her last stop at the giraffe barn — and the one animal it hurt most to leave. Ruke was in the barn today, letting the females graze alone in the enclosure. She climbed up the ladder to the top perch and sat on the railing, calling him over with a handful of lettuce.

"Hey, boy," she greeted, letting him take the treat. "I saw your girl out there. Gonna have a little one soon, huh?" Lady Regal was certainly pregnant, and Evangeline was a little bummed she wouldn't be around to see the baby being born. "I guess it's true when they say that time heals all wounds."

Then she sighed, wondering if that was true in her case as well. And if so, how much time? She did feel better now than she had in the past six months, but that didn't mean the nightmares had stopped, or that she was able to push away the dark memories of that day.

"I hope it's true," she answered her own unspoken question. "I don't want you to think I'm leaving you too, buddy. It's just that, my time here is up and I have to go back to real life, I guess. I don't really want to go back, but I don't have a choice. But you have to keep on being your grumpy but happy self. You can't go back to moping around and being depressed … And neither can I."

Ruke nudged her hand and reached out with a purple tongue, nearly licking her on the chin before she chuckled and pulled back. "Yeah, yeah." She pulled out a handful of small branches with leaves on the ends and fed them to him one by one. "I wish I didn't have to go. I'm gonna miss you."

"He's gonna miss you too."

Evangeline didn't need to look to know who had joined her in the barn. She waited for Caster to climb up to the railing, where he sat down next to her. "I wish I didn't have to go."

Caster frowned at her repeated statement, thinking back to all the teenagers who had come to the preserve over the years. "Just about everyone says that. They all leave though. Sometimes I wish they could stay. Certain people, anyway."

Shooting him a curious stare, Evangeline said with a grin, "Like me, clearly. You'll be lost without my cheery presence." They both laughed, breaking whatever tension in the air that had formed when he entered the barn. "You better not paint over my mural."

"Never," Caster agreed, surprised when Ruke shifted his attention to him and allowed him to pet his neck. "You've really done a number on this guy. I can't believe how much better he is."

"Well, hopefully he stays better. He's got a baby on the way, after all. What will you do with the baby, anyway?"

"Not sure." Caster shrugged. "Jett is still working on getting some connections with a wildlife preserve in Africa. They have programs for reintroducing animals into the wild and I'm sure they'd be interested in an infant, especially if it's a male. Ruke and Lady Regal both have great bloodlines."

The thought of Ruke and Lady Regal having their baby shipped off saddened her, though she knew it was the way such things worked. "Sometimes it seems like everyone leaves, or is taken away," she said softly.

Caster bumped her shoulder with his own. "You've still got us. Just like you've got Jett and Lettie. You've always got a home here."

Jett echoed that same sentiment only hours later, when he dropped her off at the airport.

"You stay out of trouble and you do good things, ya hear me?" he said after releasing her from a tight hug.

"I hear ya," Evangeline answered around a sniffle. She didn't want to leave, didn't want to give up the happiness she'd found with him and the animals. "Give Ruke a hug for me."

"I'll do my best. That grump only likes you," Jett

chuckled. "You let me know if you need anything, okay? You got someone picking you up on the other side?"

"Yeah, my mom." That surprised them both.

"Well …" Jett reached into his back pocket and pulled out an envelope. "This is for you. Some cash for the road and the rest, well, do something good with it."

Evangeline took the envelope and looked inside, eyes widening at the green bills and substantial number on the check. "I … I don't understand. I can't accept this. It's way too much money."

"It's yours. The state thought it needed to pay me to take you in. I don't need money to take care of my family." Her eyes watered at the honesty in his voice and she looked down, not able to meet his gaze. "You'll take the money and that's that. I ain't taking it back."

Evangeline traced her fingers over the envelope, something close to love building in her chest. "I'll do something good with it," she promised in a whisper.

Jett nodded and took in a deep breath. Evangeline saw the tears in his eyes, didn't need to wonder about them. "Take care, little elf," he said with one more hug, and then released the girl who had become his daughter.

THE RETURN

NO ONE WAS waiting for her at the airport.

She stood outside the sliding double doors, watching people embrace their loved ones, witnessing their joyful reunions. Everyone had someone waiting for them; those who didn't eagerly headed for the vehicles that would take them to the ones waiting at home. The rush of people, a flurry of bodies greeting one another, reminded Evangeline of everything she lost.

For too long she stood there staring at people who had what she didn't — a family. Rick had promised her that her mother would be waiting, that Edith was eager to see her again.

Rick had lied.

Or, she considered as she turned back inside the airport, he was lied to.

She didn't know what to do, so she spoke with a woman at one of the ticket counters and was pointed in the right direction. Not allowing herself a moment of self-pity, Evangeline told herself to stay calm, to figure this out on her own.

She only had herself now.

An hour later she was sitting in the back of a taxi, watching the unfamiliar surroundings turn familiar the closer they drove toward home. During the drive, that dreaded self-pity threatened to creep in and she wondered what she was even doing in Florida. There was no one here for her. No one cared enough to pick her up at the airport. Edith Frost had clearly said what she needed to say to make her caseworker happy, and then promptly forgot it all. That single word Evangeline had tried so hard to forget — *unwanted* — rang through her thoughts until all she could do was close her eyes and pretend she was back in California.

Thirty minutes later they arrived at her house, the same cold structure, even colder now in the waning sunlight. Evangeline sat in the backseat, staring up at the house once called home.

"You all right back there, miss?" the driver asked when she didn't move, peering at her in the rearview mirror.

"Yeah," she answered, forcing herself to move before he could ask any more questions. She retrieved her luggage from the trunk and paid the driver using some of the cash from Jett, then started the long walk up the driveway. It wasn't really that long, but each step felt heavier than the last, dread stalling her as the house loomed closer.

Briefly she was reminded of her other long walk up this drive. Her knee was healed now, so what slowed her down wasn't pain, but fear.

Quit being a coward.

Finally, she stopped at the front door, surprised that her hand was shaking ever so slightly as she raised her key. That trembling filled her entire body as she attempted to unlock the door, only to discover the key didn't fit. Again she tried, unable to gain entry into the place that had been her home for seventeen years.

The locks, Evangeline realized with a sigh. Her mother had changed the locks while she was gone. That word — *unwanted* — rang through her mind again, but she pushed it back and forced herself off the porch. She tried all the windows, hoping for one to be unlocked, and breathed a sigh of relief when the living room window slid open. She tossed her bags in first, then carefully lifted one leg over at a time to hoist herself in the house that was no longer hers.

Evangeline didn't allow time for shame or embarrassment or even anger as she stepped inside, closing the window behind her. She stood in the living room for a moment, taking in her home, listening for sounds of life. Somewhere in the house, a television was playing.

"Mom?" Evangeline called out hesitantly, waiting a beat. When no one answered or stirred, she entered farther, leaving her bags by the window as she searched. She found the kitchen in a state of chaos, dirty dishes overflowing the sink, trash spilling out on the floor, several empty wine bottles cluttering the counter. The living room fared better, a few blankets crumpled into balls on the couch and recliner, an old TV dinner on the coffee table.

Evangeline turned away from the sight and walked deeper into the house, to her mother's room. There, she found the one she sought.

Though it was barely dinnertime, her mother lay curled up in bed atop the comforter, arms wrapped around a pillow — her father's pillow, Evangeline noted. A wine bottle was sitting on the nightstand, empty. Even from the doorway she could smell the alcohol.

Her mother shifted, sighing in her sleep, curling tighter into a ball. Evangeline moved from the doorway to the bed, lifting an afghan from a chair and resting it over her mom's sleeping body. For a moment she simply watched her sleep, taking in every inch of her face, committing the image to memory. Edith Frost was still a beauty in her own right, with her high cheekbones and full lips. Even grief couldn't take that away. And in sleep, the misery that reflected in her eyes didn't cast the rest of her face in shadows.

For so many months she'd been afraid to look her mother in the eyes, and then gone without seeing her at all during her time at the preserve. Seeing her now, in this peaceful moment, brought tears to Evangeline's eyes.

Slowly, she walked around the bed, then lay down next to her mother. If she tried hard enough, she swore she could smell her father's cologne on the sheets, in the air. Pushing those thoughts aside, she scooted closer to her mother and turned on her side so that her forehead pressed against Edith's back.

"I'm sorry, Momma," she whispered to sleeping ears. "I'm sorry I couldn't tell you the truth … I just couldn't ever say the words. I hope you're having nice dreams of Daddy."

Closing her eyes, she allowed herself to sleep.

EVANGELINE AWOKE ALONE.

She didn't know what caused her to stir, only that she opened her eyes to darkness. The clock on the nightstand read just after midnight. Rising from the bed, she left her mother's empty room and followed the light into the living room, where her mom was sitting on the couch watching a rerun of an old sitcom.

"I'm home," Evangeline said from the doorway, silently chastising herself for the obvious statement.

"I saw the bags," Edith answered without turning.

Evangeline glanced over her shoulder at her luggage, which was still next to the window in the living room. She bit back a sigh and entered the room, deciding not to ask why her mother didn't pick her up from the airport. Forgot, didn't want to, it all boiled down to the same thing.

Unwanted.

She stopped in front of her mother, lowering herself to the floor and looking up at her. "Mom, there is something I need to tell you. I never told you before, but—"

"It won't change anything," Edith cut in, eyes never leaving the TV, not even when she took a sip of wine. "The best part of my life is gone. Nothing you can say will change that."

Her shoulders slumped, Evangeline could only nod.

The silence seemed to fuel her mother. "Your things

are already packed. I expect you to find somewhere else to live by the end of the week." When Evangeline's lips parted in surprise, Edith let out a noise of exacerbation. "You're seventeen. That's old enough to start figuring life out on your own."

She brought the wine glass to her lips, ending the conversation. Evangeline rose and shuffled to the doorway, where she stood for another minute, contemplating her thoughts. No, nothing she could say would change the fact that her father was gone. She'd already decided to hide the truth and preserve her father's memory, but there was a part of her, however small, that wanted to shout it from the rooftops just so people — especially her mother — would stop looking at her like she had sucked the joy out of life itself. The truth was on the tip of her tongue, the devil on her shoulder encouraging her to abandon conviction and preserve her character.

You deserve to be absolved.

You did nothing wrong. He *caused the accident, not you.*

She's kicking you out on the street. She brought this on herself.

She became a drunk and abandoned you.

She deserves to hurt.

"He said he loves you." The words slipped out, stiffening her mother's back. Evangeline continued softly, "That day, in the car. He said he loved me, and that he loved you, and that if anything ever happened to him, to tell you that." It was a truth within a lie, but only she would know that. "I'm sorry I didn't tell you earlier, but … I thought you would like to know that he was always thinking of you, and that he loved you so much."

Evangeline kept her eyes on the floor, so she didn't see the single tear that slipped down her mother's face. Nor did she see the hard swallow that followed. Only when she started out of the room did she hear the sorrow in her mom's voice.

"Evangeline."

She stopped, one hand on the doorway, not risking a glance over her shoulder.

"You'll always be my daughter … We just can't be a family."

The words should have hurt more than they did. They should have destroyed what little happiness she had managed to find these past few months. They should have crumpled her already fragile mental state. They should have brought tears to her eyes or screams of rage to her throat. But all Evangeline could do was press forward, and accept that she was alone.

MAKE A DECISION

A CLOSED DOOR at the end of the hall met her sight, an ominous vision that brought forth more trepidation than it did comfort. She opened the door tenderly, almost afraid of what she would see when the light flicked on. This room had once been her sanctuary, only to become her coffin. Would it still hold the same darkness, suffocating with memories of a broken girl?

Get over it, she told herself, then shoved open the door and flicked on the light.

Her things were packed. Actually packed, in boxes shoved alongside the far wall. Only the bed, dresser, and desk remained, all stripped bare. Evangeline scanned the room from the doorway, not surprised by what she saw. Every trace of her old life was gone.

Her mother told Rick she would prepare her room. She just never said she was preparing to kick her daughter out.

With a sigh, Evangeline entered, eventually making her way to the corner by the closet. Blood, so much blood, stained the carpet. Her blood, a reminder of her weakness, a mocking salute to death that a parent couldn't care enough about to clean.

Evangeline sat in the corner against the wall, the same position she'd been in when she attempted to take her own life. That single, life-changing act felt so long ago, part of someone else's life. She wasn't the same girl who couldn't see any other way out, a girl still a child unable to cope with the harsh realities of the world. No, she was Evangeline Frost, child forced to be an adult. The person she was now was harder, smarter, and yet, still terrified of an unknown future.

Her eyes traced over the bare walls, seeing blank white squares where her paintings used to be. Her fingers grazed over her scar, which she no longer kept covered. There was no art to surround her in a canvas of comfort, no cell phone to give access to the outside world, no memory of her father to save her.

Come morning, she would need to figure out a plan. But for now, all she could do was stare at the bare, blank walls.

WHEN THE FRONT door opened and Cam's concerned face appeared, Evangeline wasted no time asking, "Can I stay here for a few days?"

He stared at her for a few seconds, surprised by the abrupt and strange request, then shook himself out of the daze and gestured her inside. "Of course, Evie. When did you get back? What the hell happened?"

Fighting off a sigh, Evangeline set a bag down in the foyer — the rest of her stuff was already in storage using some of the money Jett had given her; she was able to figure that much out — and ran a hand through her unbrushed hair. "Short version? I got back yesterday and Mom kicked me out."

"She did what?" Cam's mother asked as she came into view. The expression in her eyes was dark, a mix of anger and sadness for the girl she'd known before the teenager could even walk. "I'm going to call her and —"

"No," Evangeline cut in. "Thank you, but no. It's done and I'm fine with it. Well, I'm learning to be fine with it," she added when Cam lifted a brow. "I just … I need a few days to figure out what to do next."

"You stay here as long as you need." Cam's mom pulled her into a hug. The embrace nearly brought tears to Evangeline's eyes. It had been so long since she'd been hugged like that, with so much love and concern, that she'd nearly forgotten what it felt like to be wrapped in a mother's arms. "Cam will get you settled in the guest room. I'll make everyone some lunch."

Evangeline followed Cam up the stairs, glancing at the pictures that lined the wall along the way. She'd always loved Cam's house, and the farm that stretched out behind it. Even if they were strict about their son's schoolwork, his parents were some of the coolest she'd ever met, painting the walls a different color every six months, filling the walls with art from local craft shows and family pictures, and always trying new foods for dinner. Her own parents were cool in their own way, but very grown up, Evangeline had always thought. At Cam's place, she felt a lot freer.

Once in the guest room, Evangeline flopped down on the bed, suddenly exhausted. It had been a long morning that involved repeat taxi trips, dealing with storage lot managers, and attempting to say good-bye to a distant mother. Cam jumped down on the bed too, bouncing her a little before settling down on his back next to her. They lay side by side staring at the ceiling, contemplating their thoughts.

"You okay?" Cam finally asked.

Evangeline crossed her arms, mouth twisting in a smirk. "I get to live on my own. Every teenager's dream, right?"

"Ya better invite me to your first party."

"Yeah, since you're my *bestie* and all." They both laughed despite the seriousness of his original question.

"Why didn't ya tell me you were coming home?"

Evangeline thought about the question for a moment. "I guess I didn't want to make a big deal out of it. I wasn't sure how Mom would react and figured I might need a few days to adjust."

Cam glanced at her out of the corner of his eye. "Guess I'll let it slide then." They were quiet another moment before he asked, "You coming to prom?"

"Wasn't planning on it," Evangeline sighed. "I barely know anyone there anymore and I'm not even technically a student. Who you taking?"

Cam shrugged. "Jenny Keegan. No big deal."

"No big deal?" She glanced over at Cam, who was trying hard to keep a straight face. "You've been asking her out since the fifth grade. You mean she finally caved? Why?"

"Hey, I can't help it if I'm irresistible."

"Guess it just took her seven years to realize that, huh?"

"Shut up."

"Y'all are awfully quiet up there!" Cam's mother shouted from the base of the stairs. "Do I need to be worried?"

"Only if ya don't want grandkids!" Cam shouted back, earning a smack on the shoulder from Evangeline and a snort from his mother.

"Please. Our Evie has good taste."

Evangeline cracked up at his mother's response, ignoring the elbow Cam jabbed into her ribs. She sat up and jumped off the bed. "Come on, let's get lunch, loverboy."

He beat her down the stairs, pausing in the hallway after glancing over at the front door, where Evangeline's single duffel bag still sat. The zipper had pulled down some at one end, revealing a few inches of brown speckles.

"What's this?" he asked, walking over to the bag and pulling out the item. A cheesy grin spread over his face when Evangeline chewed on her bottom lip in response. "Do I give the best gifts or what?"

Evangeline stalked over and snatched Jengo the Giraffe out of his hands. She cuddled the stuffed animal to her chest. "So what? You gonna make a big deal out of it?"

Cam lifted a brow, amused. "No."

"Good."

He wanted to tease his childhood friend, but seeing her standing there with the giraffe clutched against her touched his heart a little. He wasn't comfortable with that emotion, so he shrugged it off by shoving her shoulder. "Put down the giraffe and back away. I'm hungry."

Grateful for the escape, knowing he gave her the out because he really did care, Evangeline did just that and followed Cam into the kitchen, the two pushing each other into the walls along the way.

"SO YOU'VE BEEN at Cam's for two weeks now?" Rick asked as he settled down in his office chair. Evangeline sat across from him on the couch. She looked better, he noted with satisfaction. Tanner, more weight on that formerly skinny frame, hair actually brushed. "How has that been?"

"Fine. He annoys me, but he's like my brother so I guess that's to be expected. His parents are cool with it for now, but I'm sure they want me out."

"Have they said as much?"

"No. I'm just guessing." She knew his parents liked her, but hospitality had its limits and she didn't want to overstay her welcome.

"Have you spoken to your mother again?" When the girl only lifted a brow his direction, Rick conceded. He already knew how things were going at Cam's, as he'd spoken with the boy's parents the day she'd shown up on the family's doorstep. It was his job, though Evangeline's age did put her at a disadvantage. He was willing to go above the call of duty for her. "How are you doing with that? With your … separation, we'll call it."

Evangeline shrugged and considered his question seriously. "I'm fine. Really," she added when he only looked at her over the tops of his glasses. "I mean, what else am I going to be? I'm not going to fall apart again. Not over her."

His smile proved he was pleased with her answer. "I'm glad to hear it, Evangeline. And I'm sorry for what happened. I should have known your mom was just telling me what I wanted to hear. I really thought she wanted to be with you again. Or maybe I was just hoping for it that much. Either way, I'm sorry I failed you."

"You didn't fail me," Evangeline replied, honesty coating her words. "She did."

The pair was silent for a moment before Rick continued. "Are you handling things okay? There are steps we can take with your mother, considering what she—"

"No," Evangeline cut in. "I don't want her dragged through this any more than she already has been. We've both been through enough. Let's just let it go. I've been doing much better. No angry outbursts, no punching walls. I'm trying to learn to stay calm and think of happier times when I get sad."

"Sounds like you really learned a lot out at Kindred Hides."

"I did. Ruke taught me a lot," Evangeline replied with a nod, picturing the animal in her mind. "We were two of a kind, broken in our own ways. Two fragile creatures who had to be put back together again. Now, we have to move on."

"Any thoughts on what you are going to do next?"

My, he's full of questions, Evangeline thought with a frown. She'd come to see him before going to Cam's that first day, and the man had been nearly silent, letting her vent, say what she needed to say in the privacy of his office so that she didn't unleash her emotions on her mother, or anyone else. He'd known then that questions weren't what she'd needed, but rather, a safe place to feel what she needed to feel.

But fourteen days had passed since then. Since she wasn't in school — graduation had come in the form of a piece of paper and a handshake in the principal's office after passing her final exam just a week ago — and didn't yet have a job, there really hadn't been much to do other than think about what would come next. She was seventeen, creeping up on eighteen. Still didn't have a driver's license and certainly didn't have a car. Once she planned on going to school for art, but that seemed like such a pipe dream now.

"I don't know," she finally admitted. "Cam wants me to wait for him to graduate, then we can get a place as roommates while he goes to college. He and his parents think I should start doing commission work again for my paintings. I used to bring in pretty good spending money."

"And what do *you* want to do?"

What did she want? Did she want to go to college or get a job close to home, like Cam? She loved Cam and his family, but living in this town would suffocate her, especially knowing she might run into her mother at any given time. Did she want to paint? She could hold the brush again with only a minor amount of pain. Did she want to move somewhere else and completely start over? The thought was terrifying.

So what did she want to do? More importantly, what did she want out of her life, period? What would make her happy?

"Evangeline? Do you know what you want?"

Her grin was answer enough.

36

A HOME TO HEAL

CASTER MET JETT and Lettie in the office, wondering what he'd been summoned for. It was already midday and he had a lot of work left to do. Jett still hadn't replaced Ash, and even Evangeline had put in a good share of work during her time. The entire preserve was feeling the loss.

It surprised him that he missed the girl who'd been a complete pain in his ass. He normally didn't like socializing with people not part of the preserve, and especially didn't get too close to those part of the Second Hides Program, even though he'd been part of it once himself. It was easier getting along with the animals.

"What's up?" he asked as he entered the office. Jett was behind his desk, reading glasses perched on the end of his nose and some sort of paperwork in hand. Lettie sat across the desk from him in one of the uncomfortable guest chairs. She gestured for him to take the seat next to her.

"Caster, hey," Jett greeted, setting down the papers and regarding him with a strangely serious expression. "I wanted to talk to you regarding a couple changes."

His uncle's tone had Caster worried. "You firing me or something?"

"Of course not," Jett replied as Lettie let out a laugh. "But you are a big part of the preserve and these changes will affect you the most. So." He picked up a pen and pad of paper as though reading from a checklist. The move, combined with his glasses and the gray working its way into his beard, gave him a business-like aura Caster wasn't used to seeing from him.

"First, we are taking on three new employees. One will take Ash's place with the big game mammals. The other will probably work in all areas, but I would like to have them help with the giraffes with Ash being gone."

"Okay," Caster replied slowly. Jett didn't typically consult with him on new hires. They just kind of showed up and let him know they were ready to work. "What's this got to do with me? And why are we hiring three? We only need one."

"We're hiring three because one is going to take your place."

"What?!" Caster leapt up. "You said you weren't firing me!"

Jett held up a hand, grinning widely. "We aren't. I just wanted to freak ya out." He waited until Caster sat again, arms crossed. "I'm serious in that one will take your place, but that's because you're needed elsewhere." He slid a piece of paper across the desk, gesturing for Caster to look.

Caster leaned over and scanned the paper, not knowing what he was reading until he saw one word: *Africa.*

"Africa?" he repeated. "You worked out the deal?"

"Signed the papers and faxed them over this morning," Jett said with a wide smile. "Kindred Hides Conservation of Zambia, in partnership with Kenya, is officially established. And we want you to be our representative, which means you'll be taking trips out to the African preserve and working with the conservation teams to help save the endangered populations. Eventually we will work with their breeding program, but for the immediate future we are going to focus on raising awareness regarding conversation."

The news thrilled Caster. They'd been working on this new program for almost five years, and it was finally coming to fruition. "This is amazing, Jett. This will open up so many opportunities for our preserve. And for the animals. I can't wait. When do I make my first trip?"

"About four months, after you finish getting all your shots." Jett handed him a folder. "This has everything you need to know. Read up on it, let me know if you have questions."

Caster took the folder and opened it, glancing through some of the files. An envelope was stuck to the inside flap. Inside, he found plane tickets. "There are three tickets. Who is going with me?"

"I am going with you the first few trips, to make sure everything goes smoothly, that you learn the lay of the land, everything is set up for us, and so on. I wouldn't send you off on your own without being there during the initial trips."

Caster didn't mind, since the thought of going alone certainly made him nervous. "Okay, so who is the third ticket for? Lettie?"

"No, Lettie here has to keep watch over the preserve and its motley crew while we're gone. The other ticket is for the third employee."

Caster frowned at Jett's response, along with the knowing grin Lettie shot his way. "Uh … you're sending me to Africa with a newb?"

"I wouldn't exactly call myself a newb."

The voice came from the doorway; Caster spun around to meet its owner. Evangeline stood just inside the office, arms crossed, genuine grin spread across her face. Bilbo sat perched on her shoulder, picking at her hair, his yellowish-green tail wrapped around her neck. She entered the room, still limping slightly but not nearly as badly as when she first arrived at Kindred Hides.

"Caster, I believe you've met our newest employee."

CASTER AND EVANGELINE walked to the giraffe enclosure, on equal ground. She was already dressed in work clothes, ready to pull her own weight as part of the preserve. But he had some questions to be answered first.

"So, your mom. What does she think about you coming back out here?"

Evangeline pressed her lips together. One hand absently lifted to pet the monkey still attached to her shoulder. Bilbo had taken one look at the girl when she walked into the big house and leapt from Derek to her, refusing to part with his new friend. "My mother kicked me out and disowned me. She doesn't give a crap about me working here. I doubt she even knows I'm here."

It was said so matter-of-factly that he knew better than to press the issue. "What about college?"

"Who says I can't still go?"

They stopped at the fence. Lady Regal stood at the far end of the enclosure, belly swollen with the promise of youth. Ruke came over to investigate the duo. Evangeline reached out and rubbed a hand up and down his forehead, a silent conversation with an old friend.

"What about Cam?"

"He's got his life back home. New school, pretty girl-friend."

Evangeline giggled when Ruke searched her hands for treats and ended up licking her neck with a slimy tongue. Bilbo chittered in response, annoyed by the slob-ber that was now coated on his tail. The giraffe ignored him and nudged Evangeline's shoulder with his massive head as though asking for attention. *Or demanding it*, Caster thought.

"You really want to go to Africa? Deal with the swel-tering heat, get all the medical shots, potentially deal with poachers and lions that want to eat you?"

"I get to help animals," Evangeline replied, leaning over to rest her head against Ruke's. Disturbed from his perch, Bilbo jumped from her shoulder onto Caster's and took hold of his unruly hair. "Rick asked me what I want-ed to do, what would make me happy, and I kept thinking of this place. I love the preserve and I want to keep being a part of it."

He believed her, believed the sincerity in her voice. She was young, but had been through tragedies that forced her to grow up and know what she really wanted out of life. And standing there, one arm wrapped around a giraffe's neck, that same grumpy giraffe allowing his only real human friend to do so, he knew Evangeline had found her home.

"You'll be happy here?" Caster gave her a sidelong glance. She returned his look with a smile of her own.

"I already am."

EPILOGUE

A STEP FORWARD

THEY SAT NEXT to each other on an uncomfortable bench while they waited, each lost in their own memories of the past year. Her — two parents lost by the same circumstance, finding a new family among strangers. Him — seeing a dream come to fruition, sharing his vision with someone whose eagerness both surprised and calmed him.

"So …" Caster started, unnerved by the silence and even more so by the day ahead. "Have you spoken to your mom since you came back to Kindred Hides? Did you tell her that you were leaving the country for a while?"

Evangeline stared at the ground, at the cracks that lined the concrete. "I mentioned it when I called her a few months ago for our whole forty-second conversation. But … nothing's changed. We are just two different people with too much bad blood between us. As far as I'm concerned, Jett and Lettie are more my family than Edith Frost."

It was a sentiment she'd never admitted until now, though she felt it before she left Kindred Hides, returning to a home that was no longer home. It had been months since Evangeline returned to the preserve, months that had given her time to heal, to overcome the darkness that threatened to engulf her heart, but her mother remained trapped in her grief. Evangeline didn't call her anymore after that last brief conversation, unable to bear the sounds of wine pouring into glass, the slur of distracted comments, and harsh sting of words that reminded her she was no longer a daughter, instead an orphan.

Not an orphan, she reminded herself. She had Jett, who was willing to be as much a father as she would let him, and Lettie, who was the strength her heart needed to move on.

"I went to his grave," Evangeline admitted then, her voice a mere whisper. "Just before I left Florida for good. I'd never gone before. It was … scary, but I think it helped. I got to say all the things I wanted to say, but never had the guts to do before."

He didn't ask what she said. Such words were too personal to even inquire about. But he did ask another question. "Did your mom go with you?"

A sarcastic laugh escaped Evangeline as she sat back against the hard plastic and squinted in the bright morning sun, nerves twisting in her gut. She wasn't sure what was worse, talking about her mother or how ridiculously nervous she was at what they were about to do.

Definitely the mother stuff, she thought, deciding she

was more excited than nervous about the day soon to come.

"Yeah, right," she answered Caster. "No, Cam went with me. We both had some things to say, needed that closure."

"And how is Cam?"

She heard the sarcasm in his question, but didn't acknowledge it. The guys were weird around each other, what few times Cam had visited Kindred Hides after she returned. It didn't matter that the love of his life, Jenny, was in tow. Evangeline chalked it up to boys being boys.

"Cam is ... Cam. Loves being on his own, adjusting to college life. Got himself a girlfriend, same girl he's been lusting after since middle school. You met her. He's infatuated with the chick." Evangeline laughed to herself, thinking of the couple. "They are really cute together. I'm happy for them." And she was. Her family had caused her childhood friend enough grief, and she hoped Cam could move forward now, into a brighter future.

"And what about you?" Caster stretched his arms across the back of the bench, staring out through the glass windows in front of them at the bustling traffic.

Evangeline shrugged. "I'm adjusting," she answered, glancing down at her hands. "Sometimes I still forget Dad is gone and I want to call him and tell him a joke I heard. Or I think about sending Mom a birthday card and remember she will probably just throw it away." She was quiet for a moment, reflecting. "When I was a kid I had a totally different version of my life. Go to college, study art, become a professional artist who travels around the country doing craft shows and painting on commission. I even sketched out my future house once, with a huge painting studio." She shook her head at her own foolishness, observing her right hand. It still hurt to hold a brush, or anything really, but it was getting better, one hand massage at a time. "So much for that, huh? Guess I have a new life now."

Caster started to reply, to tell her that her life could still be any and everything she'd ever dreamed it could be, but his words died in his throat. He wanted her to still have those dreams, and yet, he also wanted her to envision her life with the preserve. He didn't know the child or teenager she once was, the goals she'd set for herself at such a young age, but he knew the woman she was now — the kind of woman Kindred Hides needed.

He started to reply, to tell her she could still do all those things, but was interrupted when Jett appeared, a large pack slung across his shoulder and a wide smile spread across his face, barely contained behind his bushy black beard.

"You kids ready?"

Caster and Evangeline stood, gathering the bags at their feet. They fell into step behind Jett, anticipation building in their chests, grins forming at the blast of heat that pushed against them when the double doors slid open.

Caster looked over at Evangeline, saw the eagerness in her eyes. "Any regrets about your new life?"

Her eyes sparkled in the morning sun when she glanced over at Caster. "None at all," she replied, tightening her grip on her backpack and moving forward when Jett called over his shoulder at them to hurry up.

Together they followed his direction, stepping out of their old world and into Africa.

THANK YOU!

Fragile Creatures was a new kind of book for me, one not filled with swordfights, gangs, magic, suspense … basically all the things I'm used to writing. No, this one was rooted in our world, a story meant to touch the heart, and, let's face it, I'm not exactly a sentimental person – except that I do absolutely love animals.

So, it is with complete honesty that I say this book would not have been possible without the help of several readers and fans. Their feedback on the story helped make the book that much better. I specifically want to thank the following people:

My momma, Cindy, for her invaluable insight into the Second Hides Program and how such a setup would work. Also, for her insistence that I am capable of writing a feel-good story.

My father, Rytch, for more invaluable insight into Evangeline's move to the preserve and advice on how a parent would react. Good thing I let him read this copy in advance. :)

My street team folks who read early versions and offered advice on areas to improve and showed such excitement about the final version that even I was a little giddy. Specifically, I want to thank Stephanie North, Donna Dull, Mackenzy Dodds, Kathy Corbett, Kristi Strong, and Amy Jones.

My amazing editor, Juli Valenti of Juli's Elite Editing, and outstanding formatter, JT Formatting. You two make my books shine like never before!

Michelle Monique for an absolutely amazing cover. Seriously, 'beyond talented' doesn't even begin to describe her. Plus, I gotta give her props for totally making it happen when I said, "I don't know how to do it, and everyone else said it couldn't be done, but I want a giraffe on the cover."

Rick Miles, my awesome PR agent, for helping me promote this novel and others while walking me through a lot of marketing projects that, frankly, I'm too lazy to do on my own. Circelli Books is taking on a new life with his help!

All of my talented indie author friends for their constant support. Whether we're talking about books, day jobs, or life in general, I can always count on them to listen and laugh or be outraged on my behalf. Kristi Strong, Donna Dull, Amy Jones, Dawn Pendleton, Magan Vernon, Bethany Lopez, Bonnie Paulson, Brenda Rothert, Andrea Heltsley, M.r. Polish, Christie Rich, Erin Danzer, Susan Burdorf, Julie Titus, Ashley Lavering, Jennifer Snyder, Alyssa Rose ivy, Heather Teresi Lyons, Jill Cooper, Sarah Ashley Jones – y'all rock!

And, of course, all my readers. Thank you for continuing to read and support my books. I hope you enjoyed *Fragile Creatures*!

ABOUT THE AUTHOR

KRISTINA CIRCELLI IS the author of several fiction novels, including *The Helping Hands* series and *The Whisper Legacy*.

Her latest series, *The Whisper Legacy*, features *Beyond the Western Sun*. This book is what all fantasy adventures must strive to be: a complex, intricate examination of human emotion set within the context of worlds known only in our imagination. Melding fantasy and legend in an epic quest, this series signals the arrival of Kristina Circelli as a master storyteller and an important voice in Native American literature.

A descendent of the Cherokee nation and niece of a Cherokee elder, Circelli holds both a Bachelor of Arts and Master of Arts in English from the University of North Florida, where she also teaches creative writing.

To find out more about Kristina and her books visit:

http://www.circelli.info

OTHER BOOKS BY KRISTINA CIRCELLI

The Whisper Legacy:

Beyond the Western Sun
Walk the Red Road
Into the Shadow Realm

The Helping Hands Series:

The Helping Hands
Shadows in the Night
The Iron Fist: Legacy of the Helping Hands
Abandon

Standalone Novels:

The Sour Orange Derby
The Never
Fade into the Woodwork

Short Stories:

Dungeon